Destination P

Edna Forrest

First Published 2005

ISBN 0-9543407-4-4
Published by
MM Publishing
Longridge
Sawbridgeworth Road
Hatfield Heath
Bishop's Stortford CM22 7DR

Printed by
Inky Little Fingers www.inkylittlefingers.co.uk

Design and Typesetting
by Diane Parker

Cover photo supplied by Monica Ryan, CWE Creative
www.cwecreative.moonfruit.com

For Jock

My grateful thanks to my severest critics... our daughter Gillian and son-in-law Bill.

Thanks also to Diane Parker and Monica Ryan, CWE Creative

Chapter One

The tyres on the shiny, sleek, silver Mercedes screeched to a halt at the quay side, throwing the passenger sharply forward.

"Sorry Miss." The liveried chauffeur smiled apologetically. "In a bit of a rush."

"Don't upset her, John. She could do you an injury."

The voice coming from the depths of the back of the car was sarcastic and Georgina wriggled uncomfortably as she remembered the scene back at the garage where she had left her broken down car.

Georgina's Irish ancestors had not only bestowed upon her the name of Murphy, a pair of dancing, dark green Irish eyes, shaded by long black lashes which swept down on to a face with a complexion as delectable as peaches and cream. They'd also passed on to her an explosive, gallic temperament that she tried, not always with success, to keep under reasonable control.

Georgina had accepted a lift to Southampton dock where she was to join the Cruise Director's team on the Starlight's world cruise.

She half turned in her seat to respond, but the chauffeur smiled at her.

"Come on girl. You're gonna miss this ship if you don't get a move on. I'll give you a hand with your luggage"

"No thank you. I don't have much. Most of it has gone on ahead so I don't need any help."

Adam Reynolds spoke again, this time his voice rough and impatient.

"Then for God's sake get out."

Nineteen year old Georgina Murphy lifted her case from the boot and started to walk away. She turned to look back at the car and as she did, she saw Eve Reynolds lean over and kiss Adam on the cheek. She hesitated for a couple of seconds, then strolled back to the car and knocked on the window. The woman opened it, staring at Georgina disdainfully.

"Well?"

Georgina leaned past her, catching as she did the scent of a very expensive perfume.

"Nice arse, Adam," she whispered seductively.

She turned and walked towards the gangway with a smile of satisfaction hovering on her lips, confident that she had left Adam Reynolds to face an uncomfortable session with his wife.

Georgina approached the gangway, staring in wonderment at the cruise liner berthed alongside the quay. She could hardly believe that this great blue and white vessel was to be her home for the next three and a half months. The decks were filled with masses of people, throwing out streamers and balloons, waving their goodbyes to the crowds filling the viewing platforms on the quayside. Standing on either side of the gangway, were uniformed crew waiting to welcome passengers aboard although by this time most of them had already arrived. All luggage had been dealt with by the porters and would now be being placed in the cabins.

It was six on a miserable, rainy January evening. A cold and damp brass band and a group of Scottish pipers were grouped ready to play. Soon the Starlight would leave her moorings to be guided out into the darkness of the English Channel by tiny tug boats, heading for the exotic venues of Costa Rica, Acapulco, Honolulu and many others with much sunnier climes than she was leaving behind. There was an air of excitement and anticipation that only the departure of a great liner can create, and dancer Georgina had to pinch herself to realise that she was going to be part of it all.

"Pass please, Miss." A young officer examined her papers and handed them back to her with a smile. "You gonna be one of 'Pete's people?"

Georgina looked confused. "Who's Pete?"

"Cruise Director."

"Erm... yes. I suppose I am."

He handed back her papers and smiled. "Great. I'll be seeing a lot more of you then."

Georgina continued up the gangway, oblivious to the admiring glances of the other officers. She was very aware that her petite, perfectly formed figure, her mass of blue-black hair curling softly around her face and cascading down on to her shoulders, made her a target for open hostility from many a woman and won admiring glances from many a male. But Georgina was sufficiently street-wise to recognise danger and her profession as a dancer in West end shows had given her the confidence to ward off unwelcome amorous advances. And anyway, she was immune to men for the time being. At least, she thought she was, but her confidence had been shaken by the man in the back of the limousine. Adam Reynolds. Tall and dark. Piercing, hazel eyes. Athletic body. Not handsome but very, very attractive.

Once on board, Georgina was suddenly unsure of what to do next. This was new territory for her. She was in unfamiliar surroundings and not aware yet

of her status in what at the moment was an alien environment. Every one looked so busy, she was loath to interrupt. So she leaned on the rail of the ship, savouring the moment of departure, listening to the conversations of people around her. A young couple with a baby, excitedly making plans for a new life in Sydney, and waving joyfully to what looked like weeping parents on the quayside. A middle-aged man and woman heading for Perth looking forward to a months stay with their family and seeing grandchildren for the first time. A honeymoon couple on their way to Singapore, rapturously engrossed in each other. Lots of elderly women milling around, seemingly looking to forge relationships right at the start of the cruise and a smattering of males making a quick exit whenever a female approached. Georgina viewed the scene dreamily, her vivid imagination concocting stories about the people surrounding her. Jerking her rudely out of her reverie, the ship hooted sonorously, saying goodbye to Southampton and warning other vessels of its imminent approach. Someone pushed a handful of streamers in her hand, the band started to play "There'll always be an England, followed by "We are sailing," and the crowds started cheering Some of them were crying, so Georgina cried too, although she didn't know why. As the cheering reached its crescendo, the huge vessel began her journey smoothly and majestically. The crowds fell movingly silent as the music faded into the distance, the tugs said their farewells and headed back home. Starlight was on her own, ready to defy all the elements that nature could throw at her.

"Which one do you want?" Jenny, Georgina's cabin mate, smiled at her as she bounced up and down on the lower bunk. "If you're not a good sailor you'd better have the bottom one."

"I don't know whether I'm a good sailor or not," replied Georgina, hesitantly. "This is my first trip."

"Have the bottom one then. By the way, the rule is, if the waste bucket's outside, stay out."

Georgina looked puzzled. "Stay out. Out where?"

"Christ, it is your first trip, isn't it? It means I'm entertaining. You know. It means I've a fella, stupid. Same goes for you."

Georgina blushed as she realised what Jenny meant.

"Oh, no. I won't be entertaining. I have - responsibilities. I mean - I'm not into men at the moment."

Jenny laughed. "Well, suit yourself. Just stick to the rules and we'll get along fine. Now, I'll toddle off and give you some space to unpack. I've finished mine. I'll come back for you in an hour and show you round. There's to be a meeting in the board room with Pete - he's our cruise director. He'll be dishing out the duties for tonight. See you later. Oh, you'll find your uniform in your wardrobe. You must change into it. Hope you've not put on any weight since you gave the company your measurements."

The cabin door closed behind her and Georgina slowly began to unpack, taking stock of the cabin as she did so. This was to be her home for the next three months. It was much smaller than she had anticipated, but compact. In addition to the two bunk beds, there were two wardrobes, two chests of drawers, a small dressing table with drawers down one side and a radio beneath it at the other side. She opened all the drawers, thankful that Jenny had very fairly left her ample drawer space. It would be terrible, she thought, to have a selfish cabin mate. She thought about the rules of the waste bucket and sighed. Jenny's sexual activities were her own affair and who was she to moralise to anyone?

"Perhaps I should have told the truth." Georgina sat down heavily on the edge of her bunk bed, recalling her interview for this job.

Georgina had been dancing since she was four years old and her years of training had been years of exquisite delight. She'd learned with enthusiasm the intricate movements of ballet, endured the rigours of tap dancing and the excruciating manoeuvres of acrobats. She'd performed in front of audiences with unselfconsciousness and vivacity, entering competitions, expecting to win and usually did, but without pomposity, so retaining the friendship of the rest of the class. A perfect candidate for the job.

At the end of her interview for her job on the ship, Robert Barnes, Head of Entertainment had said, "I don't suppose you have any encumbrances, Georgina."

"Oh no," she answered brightly. "None at all. I'm - a free agent."

"Good."

Georgina had shivered as he'd rubbed his hands together and smiled at her. There'd been no warmth in his smile and she knew then that this man would be ruthless in all his dealings.

"I like my staff to be single minded."

Georgina delved into one of her suitcases and took out a silver-framed photograph and gazed at the picture of a little girl dressed in a tiny tu-tu, her head, a mass of deep auburn curls, charmingly tilted to one side, as she posed for the photographer with all the confidence of a professional.

Georgina gently kissed the photograph, sighing deeply. "I'm doing it all for you, Rosie."

The navy blue uniform, with its straight skirt, tailored jacket and crisp white linen shirt fitted her tiny, trim figure neatly and as she twisted this way and that in front of the mirror, excitement welled up inside her, This was going to be the start of a new life for her.

"Ready?" Jenny opened the door. "Hey, you look great."

She picked up the navy blue tricorn hat which was sitting on the dressing table awaiting its new owner and perched it on Georgina's head. Standing back to survey, she fingered the blue-black, curly, shining locks of hair which cascaded down on to Georgina's shoulders and frowned.

"I would think Pete will ask you to tie your hair back. Shame - it looks lovely. Tell you what, leave it tonight. It's a bit informal first night at sea."

The two girls, identically dressed, stood together in front of the mirror. Jenny, tall and sophisticated, her short blonde hair fitting snugly to her head. Georgina, petite, with hair as dark as night. A perfect foil for each other. They both laughed, knowing that they were going to be mates.

Georgina had difficulty keeping up with Jenny as she strode ahead of her along the labyrinth of gangways, strewn with luggage. Passengers were still boarding the ship and stewards struggled to clear the baggage and at the same time accommodate early arrivals, who were already demanding tea and biscuits. To Georgina's inexperienced eyes, it was utter chaos. She broke into a trot in an effort to catch Jenny, fearful that if she lost her she would never find her way to the board room.

"Miss - stop at *once.*"

Georgina came to an abrupt halt and turned to face the speaker. A man in uniform, whom she assumed was an officer, glared at her.

"Never run, do you hear? Never, never run."

"I... I'm so sorry. I didn't know. I... I'm new."

The man turned abruptly and continued on his way, almost bumping into Jenny as she reappeared from round the corner.

"Come *on,* George. We'll be late. What's wrong?"

"Oh Jenny, I think I'm in trouble." She nodded in the direction of the quickly disappearing uniformed figure. "That officer yelled at me for running."

"That's no mere officer, my dear." Jenny smiled. "That's the captain."

She laughed at the look of horror on Georgina's face.

"Don't *worry*. He's OK. A bit of a tyrant at times. But he's more on his mind at the moment than your running. We've only been sailing an hour. It's a busy time for everyone."

"Jenny, it's all a bit of a mess, isn't it? I didn't think we'd be ready in time. These poor stewards seem to have an awful lot to do. Can't people wait for their tea until they've finished clearing the luggage?"

"You'll find, my dear," replied Jenny, dryly, "that consideration for the staff and crew is not our passengers' concern. They are paying dearly for us to look after them and - by *Christ* - they make sure that we do."

Georgina remained silent as they hurried along. She thought that Jenny sounded very cynical. Perhaps she'd had a bad experience. Georgina made a promise to herself. She wouldn't allow anyone to antagonise her in any way. She'd keep out of trouble.

"Well, here we are again. Hi guys. Back to the grind. Hi Pete. How's Mandy? Georgina here's made a good start. She's upset the old man."

Georgina felt herself blushing as all eyes turned towards her. In spite of all her stage experience, when off stage, her tendency to blush always filled her with confusion. Someone whistled. After that, she was ignored.

Georgina looked around her shyly. Jenny was in animated conversation with a young man, casually dressed in jeans and T-shirt, and the rest of the group had gathered together, chatting, kissing, obviously meeting up again with old colleagues. Someone told a dubious story, followed by raucous laughter. Georgina knew that eventually she would become part of them, but in the meantime, she felt isolated.

"Right everyone. Settle down."

There was immediate silence and Georgina sensed that amidst the ribaldry, there was discipline and that Pete, now standing in front of them, would brook no nonsense.

"The usual duties for everyone tonight. As you know, first night out is casual. Casual for *passengers. We...*" He looked around his assembled team menacingly "... are on duty."

He nodded towards the young man dressed in jeans.

"I trust, Dave, that you intend getting your arse into something more suitable."

It was obvious that no reply was expected and Pete continued.

"We have old Mother Riley travelling with us."

There were cheers at this information.

"And - to take the smile of your faces we also have the Glums."
Moans followed this remark and Georgina realised that these were nicknames given to well known passengers.

"Please note - everyone but everyone will be given the same treatment, whatever the provocations. Remember - the passengers are *always* right. Whatever they want - within reason - they'll have. Understood?"
The company nodded silently.

"The blonde nympho is here again. No - and I repeat - no shagging the passengers - male or female. We also have one of the directors of the company cruising with us as far as Sydney so be on your guard. We anticipate rough weather in the Bay so be sure and get your arses injected if you need to. That's all, folks. Have a good trip. Jenny, look after Georgina. You're both on coffee duty in the morning."
He turned sharply and left the room.

"Anyone know the director?"
This came from Dave. There was a general shaking of heads and one by one, they left the room. A couple of them smiled at Georgina and another girl touched her hair.

"Is it dyed?"
Georgina shook her head and the girl passed through the door without further comment.

"That was Anna. Watch her. She's a jealous cow."
Jenny took Georgina's arm and led her out.

Georgina closed her eyes, allowing her body to move in tune with the unaccustomed swaying of the ship. The worries and excitement of the day were taking their toll and she had crawled into bed exhausted. Earlier in the evening, she had suggested timidly that perhaps it would be possible to have an early night. Jenny had laughed derisively.

"You must be joking girl. You'll never go to bed on the same day you get up. The *company,*" her voice was heavy with sarcasm, "will make sure that they get, just like Shylock, their pound of flesh."

The weather was already beginning to deteriorate and Georgina prayed desperately that she wouldn't suffer from seasickness, although Jenny had told her that an injection would see her through the violent waters expected in the Bay of Biscay.

"Are you a virgin?"
Startled by Jenny's question, she made no reply.

"If you are, don't let the Doc know. He's always on the look out for one. "Night, George."

Georgina lay awake, listening to Jenny's steady breathing. She'd thought that she would fall asleep as soon as her head touched the pillow, but she remained fully awake. She tried to allow the events of the day to occupy her mind in the hope that sleep would follow, but only one image emerged. A tall, dark haired man towering over her, then bending down to kiss her. Not tenderly, but roughly and with propriety. She shifted around uncomfortably, annoyed with herself.

She'd stopped for petrol and her car had refused to start. The garage owner inspected it, shaking his head.

"No good, Miss. You need a new part, I'm afraid. It'll be tomorrow at the earliest."

"But that's not good enough. You're a mechanic, aren't you? So repair it." He shook his head. "Sorry. No can do."

"Well, I'll get a taxi."

"Phew. Cost you a fortune. Anyway, they'll all be busy this time of day." He turned and walked into his office with Georgina following.

"Are there any trains?" He shook his head. "Any buses?"

"Nope."

Georgina could feel her temper rising. She *had* to get to Southampton.

"*You* take me."

"Hey, I've a business to run. Can't just drop everything."

"Well, I'll just have to thumb a lift."

The garage owner became alarmed. He'd a daughter of his own about the same age and he wouldn't want her doing that. "You can't do that, Miss." Georgina banged on the desk and tears of frustration rolled down her cheeks "Don't tell me what I can or can't do. I *will* get to Southhampton one way or another. Ah come on. Take me. I'll make it worth your while."

He was losing patience. "No," he yelled.

"Jimmy, check the spare will you?"

Georgina turned around to see a tall, deeply tanned man leaning nonchalantly by the door. His hair, almost as black as her own, brushed the collar of a dark blue polo shirt, and well cut trousers draped gently on to Gucci loafers. His hazel eyes were surrounded by long, dark lashes that many a woman would die for. A slightly aquiline nose that stopped him from being an extremely handsome man, was more than compensated by full sensuous lips.

"Right Mr Reynolds."
Picking up an oily rag, the garage owner wiped his hands, leaving them no cleaner than before. Georgina had the feeling it had been an instinctive act of deference and her fury increased.
"I'll bet he would take *him* if *he'd* broken down."
Jimmy disappeared out of the door, leaving Georgina and the man together. She moved to the door of the office awkwardly.
"Don't leave on my behalf."
He sat down in a swivel chair swinging it from side to side and smiled at her, his eyes holding hers until Georgina turned away. She felt a tingling running through her body. A tingling she hadn't experienced since she had been with a certain red headed singer called Hugh.
"Why the tears, my dear?" he asked, sarcastically. "I say, I *do* hope I'm not interrupting anything. You're a bit young for him aren't you?" He looked her up and down insolently, his smile disappearing. "Or is it that you just fancy a bit of rough?"
Georgina stared at him for a few seconds in disbelief "What on *earth* are you talking about. We weren't - I mean - I don't - it's - my car's bro... "
She stopped mid-stream. She didn't need to explain herself to this stranger. This rude, pompous bloke.
Georgina stood back and looked him up and down "You really shouldn't judge everyone by your own standards."
He completely ignored her caustic remarks. "What's your name?" he demanded.
"Murphy. Georgina. But hey. None of your business. Now, If you'll excuse me, I have a ship to catch."
"Ah, Murphy. An Irish filly. That explains the paddy."
Leaning back in the chair, he viewed her through half closed eyes and as he did so, the chair, now finely balanced on its back legs tipped over backwards and the man catapulted off, landing on all fours.
Georgina glanced appreciably at the nicely rounded buttocks clad in well-fitting, expensive looking trousers, sticking up in the air in the most ridiculous position and her sense of fun, never far from the surface swelled up inside her and she dissolved into peals of laughter.
He stood up, dusted himself down and moved towards her. Georgina stopped laughing and for a few seconds their eyes were locked in a hypnotic gaze. Slowly, he bent down from a towering height and kissed her. To her

horror, Georgina found herself responding with a rising passion.

She immediately pulled away from him and said slowly, in a deceptively quiet voice "Take your filthy hands of me before I kick your balls off."

"Hey, Miss. You could be in luck." Jimmy returned to his office, smiling his delight. "Mr. Reynolds here is going to Southampton. If you ask him nicely I'm sure he'll give you a lift."

"Of course. I'd be delighted to give the - *lady* - a lift."

"No, thank you very much."

Jimmy looked puzzled. "Thought you were desperate."

"Not that desperate," replied Georgina grimly.

"Look, do you want to catch that ship or not?"
Adam Reynolds spoke impatiently. "It's no skin of my nose but how else are you going to get to Southampton. And don't worry." His voice became heavy with sarcasm. "You won't be alone in the car with me. I do have other company."

He strode off, leaving Georgina struggling with the need to accept a lift against having to accept a favour from this moron. He might even be a sex-maniac! In the end, her desperate need to catch the ship won and, picking up her case, she followed him to the car.

"Get in. You can sit in the front with John."
Georgina peeped into the back and noted with some relief that there was indeed a woman in there. The boot of the car was open and inside were two exquisite black leather suitcases with silver monograms. Georgina looked at her own shabby case, which looked as if it had been bought at a car-boot sale, which in fact it had. Georgina sighed deeply. Since her father died, she and her mother had had to deprive themselves of the little luxuries in life to make sure that Rosie didn't go short of anything. Georgina was not materialistic for herself but she was determined that Rosie would have the best possible start in life. This world cruise was the chance of a life time and she had no intention of blowing it. Resolutely moving one of the cases to make room for her own, she caught sight of a luggage label. It read 'Adam Reynolds. Starlight.'

"He's going on the cruise." Georgina's heart missed a beat. "I'm going to see him again." She took a deep breath. "Don't be a fool," her head told her. "Think of Rosie."
She stood on tip-toe, stretching her arm to close the boot lid and paused. Who was the woman in the car? She turned over the label on the other case - Eve Reynolds. Starlight. He was *married.* The *bastard.*

“If he was *my* husband” - Georgina’s mind went into overdrive, devising ways of how she would punish him. At this stage, sleep overcame her, but she fell asleep still feeling the strength of his lips on hers.

Chapter Two

"Georgina.Wake up. Quickly."
Startled by the urgency in Jenny's voice, Georgina sat up straight, banging her head on the bunk above her.

"Ouch. Hey. That hurt. What is it. Jenny? What's wrong? Put the light on. I can't see a thing."

Jenny waved a torch frantically. "Get up. Get dressed. Something wrong with the sodding ship. There's no lighting. Even the emergency lights are out."
Georgina shot out of bed, only to be thrown back on to it.

Jenny grabbed hold of her and pulled her up roughly. "Don't piss about, George. We've gorra get out of here. We're listing badly. Hang on to something and throw some warm clothes on. Grab your life-jacket. Hold on to me. We've got to get to the lounge on the top deck. That's our designated point."

Georgina's first thought was - TITANIC. She'd just seen the film. "Ooh, Holy Mary, Mother of Jesus. We're going to die. Oh Rosie. Oh Mum."

"Oh Christ," groaned Jenny, pushing her towards the door. "Save your prayers for later. Come on - and remember," she added grimly, "passengers on the lifeboats first. And George, if we *do* sink, go down smiling. The company insist."

The lounge was already filled with worried passengers, all wearing life-jackets. Pete's people mingled amongst them reassuring them that everything was OK and officers walked quickly to and fro, adroitly avoiding answering questions.

Jenny grabbed one by the sleeve."Vince.What's happened?"she demanded quietly.

"Dunno yet. Think we might have hit something. Could be a big wave. Something's knocked out one of the generators. The power's off and we're at the mercy of the elements. The bloody ship's tossing about like a matchbox and we're in a force twelve gale. Seventy miles an hour. It's horrendous out there. Keep it quiet though. Don't want a panic."

Georgina gave a quivering sigh and shivered, just beginning to realize how ferocious the seas can be. "Jenny, I'm scared."

"You and me both," said Jenny dryly. "Listen, George. Everyone here's frightened to death. But we can't let them see that *we* are. Got to keep them calm or there'll be mayhem. Walk about and *smile* for God's sake."

"Jenny, I didn't hear an alarm. Did I sleep through it?"

"There was no alarm. Captain mustn't have thought it necessary yet, but when you've been sailing a long time, you know when something's wrong. Some passengers do too. Ships are noisy places, so when the engines stop, there's a sort of deafening silence."

For nearly two hours Starlight was attacked and buffeted by mountainous seas, that battled with this foreign object that was daring to intrude upon its domain. But, in the end, the battle was won. Starlight regained her power and although the thirty foot waves did not subside they gave way and grudgingly let her through.

The lounge was beginning to empty, passengers returning to cabins to reclaim what was left of the night and try to resume their interrupted sleep, new cruisers nervous and apprehensive, old hands declaring that they'd seen it all before and they'd not been the *least* bit worried.

"Don't believe them, Georgina. Everyone was shitting themselves." Jenny frowned. "Actually, so was I. Could have been serious. Anyway, panic over. Let's grab some kip. Early start tomorrow. Stay there, someone I have to see."

Georgina collapsed on to a large couch, sinking deep into the luxurious cushions. She was completely drained, physically and emotionally, the events of the day finally catching up with her. She had worked diligently, hiding her own fear, comforting frightened children and assuring ageing passengers that they were perfectly safe. Jenny had joined a group of officers, now relaxed and indulging in animated conversation. The lounge was empty except for a few stragglers who were hanging on in the hope of a few free drinks. Georgina felt completely alone. She closed her eyes and large, salty tears began to roll down her cheeks and soon she was sobbing quietly, wondering if she`d done the right thing in taking this job.

"Why the tears, my dear?" The voice this time was soft and concerned. She felt a gentle finger wipe away her tears. Georgina opened her eyes. Adam Reynolds was sitting by her side. "I've been watching you, Irish. You'll do fine."

"I'm so tired," she sobbed. She gazed at him through her tears, wanting suddenly to melt into his arms.

"Come here," he said gently, moving towards her, but Georgina stiffened, remembering that he was married. The last thing she needed was any trouble with an irate wife.

Pulling back immediately, he stood up and walked away, looking back over his shoulder at her. "Go to bed, Georgina."
Jenny, who'd been watching from a distance, left the group of officers and sat down beside her. "Hey. Who's the hunk? He's *gorgeous*. You're a fast worker. Think you've pulled there."

"Don't, Jenny." Georgina sighed wearily. "Come on. Let's go back to the cabin."

"Good morning, girls."
A tiny Indian steward placed a tray of tea on the dressing table and smiled broadly, showing a row of brilliant white teeth. Georgina awoke to see Jenny's long legs dangling in front of her. For a few seconds she was bemused, wondering where she was. Sitting up cautiously, remembering now to keep her head down, she viewed the tea tray with pleasure.

"Hey, I didn't expect room service."

"Course we get room service. One of the perks of the job. Don't knock it. We work bloody hard. We deserve a bit of cosseting first thing in the morning. Mind you, we don't work anything like as hard as these lads do." She smiled her thanks to the departing steward. "Poor little sods. Get paid peanuts. Depend on tips to make it worth their while and, they're away from home for nine months at a time. When we get to Goa, their families come on board to see them, but then when we leave again, they're all standing on the quayside and they're so silent as we sail away. No waving goodbye or anything. It's heartbreaking to see them. I asked him one day how he kept smiling. He pointed to his mouth and said, 'I smile here but,' he put his hand on his heart, 'I cry in here.'
Georgina smiled sympathetically as Jenny surreptitiously and impatently wiped a tear from her cheek. "Ah well that's life. Can't afford to get sentimental in this job."

She slid deftly to the floor, lifted the lid of the teapot and, stirring the tea, picked up the silver picture frame.

"What a little poppet. What's her name?"

"Er... Rosie."

"Aw, she's gorgeous. And that *hair*. I'll bet she was a surprise for your mum."

Georgina raised her head. "What do you mean?"

"Your little sister. She looks like you. There must be quite a gap between you two. Unless there's more in between, of course."

“Yes - she was a surprise and - no - there’s no more in between.”

“Your turn tomorrow.” Jenny poured out two cups of tea.

“Of course. Jenny, what do I wear today? ”

“Well, until we reach sunnier clime, winter skirt and shirt. We’ll be informed when to change into whites so that we all do it together. There won’t be any deck activities until we’re through the Bay. You’ll find all the doors leading to outside will be locked for passenger safety. There’s always some moron who wants to wander out to watch the elements. The swimming pools will be emptied and the gym’s not safe to use when the ships rolling so we’ll be expected to entertain and keep everyone happy. When there’s not a lot to do, the natives become restless.”

She laughed a little self-consciously.

“I sound dreadful, don’t I? Most of the passengers are really sweet. It’s just that - well - a few can be double A’s.”

Georgina looked puzzled. “What do you mean - double A’s? ”

“Arse aches, me dear. You’ll find out which ones. Come on. Out you get. You can shower first. I go first tomorrow and woe betide you if you go out of turn. Quick as you can now. I’m ready for breakfast.”

Georgina smiled to herself as she turned on the shower. Jenny might seem a bit bossy, but she felt that she understood her. There was no malice in her. She was lucky to have been allocated her as a cabin mate.

Jenny decided that they would dine in the staff quarters this morning so that George, as she was now known, could meet other members of the staff, some of whom were not allowed to dine in the passenger restaurant. The hair-dressers, shop assistants, some entertainers had all their meals in the staff quarters, but Georgina and Jenny, along with others members of the Cruise Director’s team were expected to mingle with passengers as much as possible, including sitting with them at dinner.

The ship was now pitching wildly, with inky-black waves rolling to a great height then breaking into aquamarine topped with frothy chantilly lace, but Georgina, delighted to find that the movement was not affecting her, ate a hearty breakfast of bacon, egg and sausage. Jenny had a cup of coffee and a cigarette and watched Georgina eat with an amused expression.

“Thought you were hungry.” Georgina reached out for another piece of toast.

“George, by the time you reach the end of this cruise, you’ll be so sick of food you’ll never want to eat again. And if you carry on eating like that, you'll have hips the size of an ox. Food is one commodity that's always available."

The atmosphere around the table was warm and friendly and nearly everyone stopped to speak to Georgina.

"You're the only new girl on this trip. And you're pretty. The men'll spoil you rotten. Why don't you have a wander for an hour? Find your way about the ship. Most passengers will feel lost this morning and soon you're bound to have some of them asking you where things are. You'll feel a fool if you have to tell them that you don't know either. And George - be professional. Don't talk about the front and the back of the ship. Or the pointed end and the blunt end. It's fore and aft. And it's starboard and portside, not right and left." Jenny laughed and shook her head at Georgina's bewilderment. "This company's a swine for not giving more training before sailing. They really do throw everyone in at the deep end. Metaphorically speaking, of course. Don't worry. You'll soon get the hang of it. See you in the Starlight Lounge. That's where coffee's being served. Remember, we're on coffee duty this morning."

Georgina took Jenny's advice and, sure enough, after a few false starts, she began to understand the geography of the ship and was able to find her way around quite easily. She was even able to direct an old lady to her cabin. Feeling pleased with herself, she hummed a tune as she made her way to the Starlight Lounge.

"My, my. A happy little soul. You're new, aren't you? Pleased to meet you. My name's Scott. Robert Scott. I'm the ship's doctor."

Georgina stopped suddenly in her tracks and looked up to see a bearded figure, resplendent in a gold braided uniform smiling down at her. But Georgina, recalling Jenny's cryptic remark that the doctor would be on the look out for virgins. involuntarily stepped back, shrieked and completely ignoring the Captain's dire warning, turned and ran, leaving the doctor staring at her fast disappearing figure with complete and utter bewilderment.

Arriving at the Starlight Lounge breathless and feeling a bit of an idiot, Georgina was confronted by a melancholy looking couple. The woman, her hair pulled tightly away from her face and wearing a drab, ill fitting cardigan and a shapeless skirt which did absolutely nothing for her skinny frame, poked Georgina on the shoulder.

"Where's the coffee?"

"Yes, where's the coffee?"

The man, his stomach bulging under a multi-coloured T-shirt and wearing a base ball cap informing the world that he had visited Miami, poked Georgina on her other shoulder.

"It's always late on this ship," sniffed the woman.

"Yes, it's always late on this ship," repeated the man.

"Morning. How wonderful to see you back again. The coffee's on its way. Let me find you a nice seat where you can see the waves."

It was Jenny. Georgina turned to her, smiling gratefully. Jenny mouthed silently to her, "It's the Glums."

"Don't want to see the waves."

"No, don't want to see the waves."

Georgina watched with admiration as Jenny manoeuvred them to a table in the middle of the lounge, motioning to the waitress, newly arrived with the coffee, to serve them first. Georgina smiled as Jenny returned to her side.

"Are they always like that?"

"Fraid so," Jenny retorted cheerfully. "Now, you take portside, I'll take starboard. Make sure everyone is served, chat to a few and keep looking round in case someone is trying to catch your eye. Try not to give anyone the opportunity to complain they were ignored. Christ, it's still helluver rough."

Georgina had been averting her eyes away from the sight of the waves that pounded the ship and then retreated, as if merely to gather reinforcements for the next attack. The Captain had made an announcement on the tannoy, reassuring passengers that the 'Starlight' had been built to withstand this kind of weather and that he himself had every intention of completing the voyage. However, he also warned passengers to stay in their cabins if they felt unsteady, as the vessel was now pitching wildly and that they were in a force ten gale.

"H... how long will this last, Jenny?"

"Another day at least." Jenny looked at her closely. "You OK?"

Georgina's voice faltered. "I... I'm not sure."

"Right, lady. Down to the hospital *pronto.* Ask the Doc for an injection. You'll be as right as rain in a couple of hours. Go *on*, George." She spoke sharply as Georgina hesitated. "If you spew up here you'll be in trouble. No need for it, you see."

Georgina walked quickly to the door. She had almost made it when she was stopped by a blonde woman, leaning back in an easy chair.

"Coffee."

Georgina, holding her hand over her mouth, shook her head and began to walk away.

"Did you hear what I said, girl? Two coffees here at once. Adam, this girl is being most insolent. Report her. What's your name?"

Adam Reynolds, who had been standing with his back to her, turned and looked at her coldly. "Her name's Murphy. Well, you heard girl. Coffee for myself and the lady."

An uncontrollable feeling of nausea overwhelmed Georgina and she fled ignobly, grabbing a sick bag from one of the many placed strategically in the handrails along the gangways.

"Come on. Wakey, wakey. You should be OK now."

Georgina opened her eyes to find Jenny standing beside her with a plate of sandwiches and a pot of tea. Gingerly, she lifted her head slowly, carefully, from the pillow and sat up in her bunk. In spite of the vessel still behaving abominably, as the sea took delight in attacking its enemy again, the debilitating nausea had completely disappeared.

"Wonderful. I feel fine. Do you know, Jenny, I can't remember going to see the doctor, although I suppose I must have done 'cos my bum's a bit sore."

"Oh God," groaned Jenny. "I *told* you he was looking for a virgin. Oops - sorry. Only joking. You're a bit of a prude, aren't you George? Come on now, eat this and you'll feel even better. Trust me." Jenny patted Georgina's head sympathetically. "We've all been through it. It's the worst feeling in the world."

"What's the time, Jenny?"

"After one. You'll have to put in an appearance. Pete's been looking for you. We have rehearsals this afternoon for tomorrow's show and this evening, I'm at the Captains 'Welcome Aboard Reception.' It's for passengers doing the full cruise. It's to make them feel wanted. Canapes and drinks. That sort of thing. Captain gives a cosy speech, telling them how wonderful they all are and then they all mingle. Lots of widows spending the kids' inheritance. Most of them looking for a fella to keep them company, probably a bit of sex thrown in. Sad really. You're to do the quiz tonight. You have to compile your own questions."

"But I'm no good at quizzes," Georgina gasped. "Where do I find the questions? I would have thought the company would do all that."

"I *told* you," retorted Jenny. "The company expect you to sell your soul for them. You'll have to go to the library and search through books. You'll soon put together enough questions to see you through the trip.We all develop our own style that way, you see. The passengers like to know what to expect."

She sighed at the look of despair on Georgina's face. "Tell you what, I'll grab a bit of lunch and meet you in the library in half an hour and give you a hand."

As she turned to leave, she stopped, frowning. "It's a good job you have me for a mate and not Anna. She'd let you stew in your own juice."

Georgina smiled her thanks as she swung her legs out of the bunk.

Although there was no let up in the inclement weather, Georgina, finding her way with ease now around the ship, realised with great relief that the doctor's injection had done the trick and she was able to look out of the port-holes at the unrelenting attack of the waves on the side of the vessel with a feeling of excitement.

She longed to be out on the deck with the wind in her hair and the taste of seawater on her lips.

As she reached the library door, she hung back. The blonde woman, Adam's wife, was about to enter. She couldn't risk being seen by her yet in case she remembered that she'd been going to report her. The woman paused and looked around her, as if waiting for someone and Georgina was able to study her. She was exquisitely and expensively dressed in a pale blue woollen suit, the skirt well above her knees, showing beautifully shaped legs. She was slender and tall, made even taller by a pair of shoes with the highest heels Georgina had ever seen and she balanced on them, even though the ship was rolling like a drunken man, as if she had been born and lived all her life on a ship.

"Boy." The woman waved imperiously at one of the passing stewards. "If you see Mr Reynolds, inform him that I couldn't wait any longer."

She turned sharply on her heels, catching sight of Georgina as she did so. Stopping momentarily, she frowned, as if trying to remember something and then continued on her way.

Georgina scurried quickly into the library in case the woman should turn and speak to her. Jenny hadn't arrived yet, so Georgina turned her attention to a volume of the Encyclopaedia Britannica which unfortunately was on a shelf too high for her to reach. Stretching high on tiptoe, her finger tips not quite touching the books, she swore quietly.

"Tut, tut, Irish. Not the kind of language I would expect from a *lady.*"

Georgina knew at once who was speaking and she felt her face flushing as she recognised the emphasis on the word, lady. Breathing deeply, determined to keep her cool, she slowly turned to face Adam Reynolds. Smiling mockingly, he looked down on her. As his eyes, those incredibly piercing hazel eyes, locked into hers, she felt once again an incredibly overwhelming physical attraction. Her legs, already weak from the inept attempt to reach the high shelves, almost gave way and she sat down sharply.

Placing his hands on the arms of the chair, he leaned over her and said softly, "Would you like some help in reaching those books?"

Georgina breathed a sigh of relief and, suddenly warming to him, smiled.

"Oh, yes please."

Straightening up, he smiled sympathetically.

"It must be *dreadful* to be so tiny. I'll ask one of the stewards to bring a ladder for you."

He turned away from her and left the library without a backward glance. Georgina sat open mouthed and then, in spite of herself began to laugh. She even began to feel sorry for his wife. She was still chuckling when Jenny arrived.

"What's tickling you?"

Georgina dapped her eyes. "Jenny, you know the bloke I met in the lounge last night. He's called Adam Reynolds. His wife's a tall, blonde, smart bit. Do you know anything about them? Does the name ring a bell?"

"Reynolds, Reynolds." Jenny frowned, thoughtfully. "Ah, yes. That's the name of the director who's travelling with us. For God's sake, George, don't upset a director or we'll all suffer. So come on. Share the joke."

Georgina, immediately sober, shook her head. "It's nothing. I - can't reach the books. Could you help me, please."

After Jenny had left her, Georgina worked steadily for the next two hours, putting together a collection of what she considered to be suitable questions. Closing the books, she sighed, gazing out of the window at the still turbulent waters. It was hard to imagine that in a few hours the same sea would be as calm as a mill pond, the sun would be shining and the passengers out on the decks, soaking up the sunshine they had paid so dearly to enjoy. How lucky she was to be able to share in those same pleasures and to be paid. True, it was going to be hard work, but she had expected that. She hoped she would never become as cynical as Jenny. She even found herself mellowing towards Adam Reynolds. After all, she was just a paid servant and if he really was a director, perhaps he was entitled to have a bit of fun at her expense.

Surprised at herself for feeling so magnanimous, she tried to analyse her feelings towards Adam. Why did he have the power to fill her with desire? Why did she feel that she would be willing to do anything he asked?

"Perhaps I'm sex-starved," she thought with dismay.

Pete, the Cruise Director's words came back to her. 'We have the nympho with us.'

Her laughter, which was never far from the surface, bubbled over and she stuffed a tissue in her mouth as a passenger threw a warning glance at her. She was obviously disturbing the peace. Leaving hurriedly, she wondered what the nympho looked like. A flight of fancy took over and she decided that Mrs Reynolds was not Mrs Reynolds at all. She was the nympho that Adam had brought along with him to keep him amused.

Georgina was brought back to earth abruptly as she entered the theatre for rehearsals. They'd already started and the choreographer, usually referred to as 'the boss,' stopped the music as she entered the room.

Fixing her with a cold stare, he remarked sarcastically, "You have deigned to honour us with your presence, have you? You are so much cleverer than the rest of the company, you don't need any rehearsals, do you? You'd like to take over my job, would you? And do you consider yourself to be suitably dressed for rehearsals?"

Georgina realised with horror that she was still in uniform. Jenny had told her to change into shorts and T-shirt. Even so, she felt that she was being unjustly treated. It was only her second day. Even in the most disciplined of productions she'd never been spoken to like that. Ignoring Jenny's frantic waving, obviously entreating her not to respond, she rounded on the choreographer with a fury that surprised even herself. As her anger petered out, there was an uncomfortable silence, broken only by a giggle from Anna. The choreographer, shocked into a state of stunned stupefaction, opened his mouth and closed it again, like a fish gasping for breath.

The company shuffled closer together as if to distance themselves from Georgina. This was unheard of. The boss's word was law, never to be questioned.

"I'll deal with this. You - girl. Into the board room, *if* you don't mind."

The last few words were spoken with heavy sarcasm and Georgina, recognising the drawling, female voice speaking now with such authority, realised with a sinking heart, that she couldn't have been more wrong in her fanciful assumption that the lady was nothing more than a bit on the side.

Georgina left the board room, blinded by tears and bumped into an old lady, almost knocking her to the floor.

"Oh dear, I'm so sorry. Did I hurt you, madam? Let me take you into the lounge. Would you like a cup of coffee?"

"That would be lovely, my dear. Now don't fuss. I'm quite alright, which is more than you are. Have you been crying?"

"No - yes." Georgina found the tears welling up again at the sound of a friendly voice.

The old lady now took charge and led Georgina to the Swallow Lounge and, finding two chairs in a corner away from the crowds, made her sit down, ordering coffee for two from one of the ever present, ever hovering stewards.

"What's your name, child?"

"Georgina - well - everyone here seems to call me George."
She laughed nervously. "Not for much longer though. I'm to be sent home. As soon as we reach Madeira. I'm not the right material."

"Who says so? By the way, I'm Mrs Riley." She leaned forward and whispered confidentially, "They all call me 'Old Mother Riley."

She smiled. "They think I don't know. I don't mind. They mean well. This is my twelfth trip on the Starlight, so I'm almost one of the crew. Now, what's all this about you being sent home? Whatever have you done?"
Georgina explained what had happened. "I don't seem to have done anything right since I got the job. I'm fiery. I know that and I try not to be. But - some people just seem to rub me the wrong way and off I go. I'm my own worst enemy. Everyone says. Anyway," she added ruefully, "I've done it now. I'm to fly back home. And - I have to pay my own fare."

"That's disgraceful. Wait till I see Eve Reynolds. She'll get a piece of my mind."

"Oh *please,*" begged Georgina, alarmed. "Please - don't say anything. I shouldn't have been talking like this."

"Eve can be a nasty bitch when the mood takes her. You leave her to me. And don't you worry your pretty little head. I must go and take my afternoon nap now."

Georgina smiled sadly as she watched the old lady totter unsteadily out of the lounge. She could understand her having been christened 'Old Mother Riley'. With her grey hair fastened back in a bun and her tall, angular figure, she was the image of the old movie character and she realised also that there would be no malice intended. She was a very sweet old lady. How very different to Eve and Adam Reynolds. What a pair. And what an effect they were having on her life. First, instrumental in her arriving at Southampton in time to catch the ship and now responsible for her having to fly home. Deep down, of course, she knew that was not true. It was her own fault. She'd better start her packing. Her eyes filled with tears again as she remembered the enthusiasm with which she had embarked on this trip. Unfortunately, she seemed to have shed more tears in the last few days than she had in all her life.

"Good God, you're not still blubbing are you, Irish? What's *wrong* with you, girl? You're on a world cruise, aren't you? Be grateful."

Georgina stood up to find herself looking up into the smiling face of Adam Reynolds, and in spite of all her resolutions, she suddenly saw red.

"How *dare* you tell me to be grateful. You're a director of this company and you should be *ashamed* of yourself. I haven't been given a chance. No training, no real guidance, *nothing*. I came on this ship intending to work my guts out and now your wife, your - *Eve*, is having me sent home. She never even listened to my side of the story." Georgina was now throwing caution to the wind. She wanted to lash out, to hurt him.

"Adam and Eve," she sneered. "Did you marry her because she's called Eve or did you seek out an Eve? And does she know that you go around kissing strangers?"

Adam Reynolds stared at her, and ignoring her last remarks, asked tersely, "What do you mean, being sent home?"

Georgina sat down again, wearily.

"A flight's being arranged for me from Madeira. I'm no good."

He spun away from her sharply. When he reached the door he turned.

"Stay there," he commanded.

Ignoring his order, Georgina slowly made her way to her cabin. Meeting her steward on the way, she asked him to fetch her cases from the baggage room where they had been stored to make more space in the cabin. The heavy cabin door closed behind her and she leaned with her back against it, closing her eyes. The ship was beginning to ride more steadily and she knew that they were approaching calmer seas. She must start packing.Walking over to the dressing table, she picked up the silver picture frame.

"Sorry, Rosie. Sorry, darling. And Mum, all those hours you spent making my clothes. All for nothing."

Georgina's mother was a superb dressmaker and, unable to afford all the dresses Georgina would need for the cruise, she'd made all her clothes which had meant working long into the night at the sewing machine. There was a knock on the door and Georgina hastily replaced the photo. It would be the steward with her cases.

"Come in."

"Don't you check who it is before inviting anyone in to your cabin?"
She gasped and spun around. It was Adam Reynolds. As the door closed, he moved towards her.

Georgina stepped back, falling on to her bunk. "What do you want?` she whispered fearfully. "Don`t come any nearer or I'll scream."

"You little fool," he retorted angrily. "Stand up at once. I came here to tell you that you've been re-instated. Your job's safe enough. Just watch your tongue in future. I've saved you this time. I won't be able to do it again. You see, young lady, I'm *not* a director of the company I'm merely a paying passenger. It is my - it is Eve who is the director. You'll have dinner with me tonight."

Georgina took a deep breath and pulled herself up to her full five foot two, obviously intended to refuse but before she could say a word, Adam Reynolds said tersely, "This is not a request, Miss Murphy. As a paying passenger I'm *demanding* that you sit with me at dinner to night."
Leaving Georgina with her mouth still open, he turned and left.

"Well, George, you've certainly set the board room buzzing. In two days you've had an altercation with the Captain, upset our choreographer - he's gay by the way, so don't try using your charms on him. Anna's jealous of your hair so you've made an enemy there, not very hard to do, admitted. You've been sacked by a director, re-instated and landed yourself a prime - and I must say very sexy - dining companion. And that's another reason why Anna's so upset. She fancies him like crazy. Oh and by the way, Dave's in love with you, but don't worry about it. He falls in love with anyone new."

Georgina laughed. "Well, I haven't tried to manipulate any of those things. Honest. It's all just sort of - happened. All I want to do is make a success of this job. Jenny, what shall I wear tonight? Come on, help me choose. Oh, I'm really excited. He is dishy isn't he? I'm a bit scared though. What shall I talk about? What if I make a fool of myself."

Jenny looked at her seriously. "Georgina, a bit of advice coming up from Aunty Jen. Don't drink any alcohol. You've to do the quiz at ten tonight.

Keep a clear head. The company 'll be watching you like a hawk. You'll be a marked man, so as to speak for a while. And George, don't get involved with Reynolds, please, please, *please.* His sort are out of our class. Don't let him use you."

"What do you mean, Jenny?"

"Christ, you really are a baby, aren't you? I can hardly believe you've worked in the West End. Didn't you meet any fella's there?"

Jenny was suddenly impatient. "For God's sake, girl. He's done you a favour. He'll expect a reward. He'll have you back in his cabin and your knickers off in between pudding and coffee. Men like him don't act the Good Samaritan without wanting something in return."

Georgina was silent. She wanted to tell Jenny that she wasn't naive. That she'd had an affair that had proved disastrous. But something stopped her. She didn't want to talk too freely about her private life. Her job carried with it an extremely high salary. In addition, it was not taxable and, with no living expenses to pay, she would at the end of the cruise be able to bank a lot of money. Money that she desperately needed.

"I can take care of myself, Jenny. And anyway, Mrs Reynolds will be there. I shall be devastatingly charming to her. I shall grovel. I shall bow down to her, curtsey to her, kiss her arse if she wants me to."

Both girls dissolved into helpless laughter.

"Seriously, Jenny - thanks for caring. You're a pal. Now, what shall I wear?"

Georgina stood at the door of the restaurant and looked around. She'd no idea which was the Reynold's table. The Head Waiter walked towards her, smiling.

"May I help you, madam?"

"I'm staff, " she whispered.

The smile disappeared and his manner became brusque. "You should find out where you're sitting before you come in. I haven't time to run after you. I've passengers to look after. Who are you supposed to be with?"

"Adam... er... Mr and Mrs Reynolds."

"Who?"

"Thank you, waiter I'll take Miss Murphy to her table."

Georgina turned to see Adam Reynolds smiling down at her. With a sigh of relief, she allowed him to guide her through the dining room where he stopped at a table for two. Pulling out a chair, he motioned Georgina to sit down.

She continued to stand, looking around her anxiously. "But where's your -

where's Mrs ... "

"Georgina, sit down, *please,"* he interrupted. "You're looking very beautiful this evening."

Georgina sat down quickly, flushing with pleasure. Jenny, after inspecting her wardrobe, had insisted that she must wear a ruby-red velvet dress with a low, revealing neckline which hugged her tiny figure to perfection. A deceptively simple dress, made of course by her mother. Her glorious blue-black hair hung loosely on her shoulders, the deep waves and curls behaving exactly as they wished.

The wine waiter approached the table. "Wine, sir?"

"My usual, please."

Two menus were already on the table and handing one to Georgina, Adam began to study the other. Georgina quickly decided what she wanted and, laying down the menu, was able to study her companion. He was dressed in an immaculate black dinner suit, startlingly white shirt, but plain - no frills down the front for this man - and black bow tie. Dark, almost black hair, slightly wavy. Hazel eyes which she knew, when he lifted his head would hold her own deep green eyes hypnotically. Not a handsome man, but attractive, a deep tan indicating that he spent a lot of time outdoors.

"Probably spends all his time cruising" thought Georgina wryly.

His face was relaxed as he studied the menu and he looked much younger than Georgina had previously remembered. She speculated as to his age. Thirty? Thirty five?

"Thirty three." He raised his head and smiled at her, revealing a deep dimple in his chin.

Georgina looked away in some confusion.

"Don't worry," he laughed. "I'm not a mind reader. I've known enough women to know there are four things they want to know about a man and age is the third."

"The third?" Georgina was curious now.

"Firstly - is he rich? Well, you'll have assumed that I am pretty well off. Secondly - is he married? Well, does it really matter? And I've told you how old I am."

"But you said four things." Georgina smiled, showing even, pearly white teeth. She decided she'd play the game.

"Are you aware that this is the first time I have seen you smile? You really should do it more often."

"What's the fourth?" demanded Georgina, feeling confident. He was quite a pleasant man after all. She completely ignored now the fact that she'd been going to question the whereabouts of Mrs Reynolds, whom she'd expected to be present. Perhaps as a director, she had business to discuss with colleagues. Perhaps Adam just wanted a bit of company whilst his wife was working.

"The fourth, my dear, should be the first." He leaned towards her and whispered, "Is he good in bed?"

Georgina involuntarily pulled back dismayed, remembering Jenny's warning. She half stood up, intending to leave.

"Sit down."

His voice was sharp, authoritative and she did as she was bid.

"You shouldn't say things like that to me." She avoided his eyes. "I'm - not - you've no right. Just because I'm employed here. Just because your wife is a director doesn't give you the right ... "

Her eyes started to fill with tears and Adam groaned. "Oh Lord. Not *again.* Look - I'm sorry. I was only teasing. I was out of order. If you start crying, I shall kiss you again and you'll be the talk of the Starlight. Now, here's the waiter. Order some food, there's a good girl."

Georgina walked hurriedly to the Starlight Lounge where she was to host the quiz. The rest of the meal with Adam had passed agreeably enough, with both of them merely exchanging pleasantries. Georgina had chosen a light meal of grilled fillet of Lemon Sole and Adam, much to her surprise had decided on a vegetarian dish. She'd assumed, entirely without reason that he would have been a steak man. He hadn't offered her any wine, obviously aware that she was on duty till the early hours of the morning. At the end of the meal, he'd thanked her politely for joining him and risen from his chair, indicating that she was free to go. As she was about to leave the restaurant, she almost bumped in to Mrs Reynolds.

"Look where you're going, girl."

The woman was dressed in a glittering silver dress, a black lace shawl draped elegantly over her shoulders. Her blonde hair was beautifully coiled on either side of her head and around her neck, a necklace of diamonds and pearls that sparkled even under the dimmed lights of the restaurant.

"I'm so terribly sorry, madam."

Georgina spoke with what she hoped would sound like genuine servility. She'd no intention of upsetting this woman again.

Pete, the Cruise Director was waiting for her. He smiled as she hurried towards him and Georgina breathed a sigh of relief. She'd been unsure of the reaction of the rest of the staff to her re-instatement. A table and two chairs had been placed ready for the quiz and Dave, who was to assist her, was already seated on one of them.

"Hope you've got your questions ready, Georgina." This from Pete was a statement and not a question. She nodded, realising again that Pete was a true professional and would tolerate nothing but the highest standard in everything and from everyone.

"After you've finished here - that should be about eleven-thirty - you'll mingle in the bars and the casino. Dave here will show you the ropes. Staff meeting ten sharp in the morning. Have a good night." He turned and walked away briskly.

"Are you nervous?"

It was the first time Georgina had seen Dave since the staff meeting when Pete had remarked on his casual dress. He was a tall, pleasant bloke with a shock of light brown, unruly hair which, Georgina gathered from the way he constantly pushed it back, was a bother to him. Dressed formally in a black dinner suit, he looked entirely different to the fellow in the jeans.

"I hardly recognised you," she smiled.

"Oh, I scrub up quite well," he retorted airily. "*Are* you nervous then?"

"No, not really. I'm looking forward to it. You'll keep me right, won't you?"

"Course I will," he replied eagerly. "Georgina - George, let's have a drink later on, shall we?"

There was a cry of "Why - are we waiting?" from the assembled passengers and taking a deep breath, her voice trembling a little at first, Georgina, with increasing confidence, hosted her first quiz.

At one-thirty in the morning, Georgina wearily made her way to her cabin, barely able to keep her eyes open. She was about to put her key in the lock when she realised that the waste bucket was outside the door. The signal to say Jenny had someone in with her. Sighing deeply, Georgina hovered around the cabin. She must sleep. Where on earth could she go? Perhaps Dave was still in the bar. She was about to retrace her steps when the cabin door opened and out stepped a young officer, fastening his tunic buttons. Coughing lightly to let him know she was there, Georgina stepped aside tolet him pass. He looked up and smiled at her without any trace of embarrassment.

"Night, Georgina. Sleep well."

Jenny was sitting at the dressing table brushing her hair. "Hi. That was

Vince. I managed to get off a bit early tonight. Did you have a good night?"

"Yes. Yes, I did. Did you, Jenny?"

"Sure did. Hey George. Listen to this. One of the old biddys was standing talking to the Captain when a bloke she'd met once or twice on the deck went towards her, smiling and with hand eagerly outstretched. She gave him a frosty look and said loudly, 'Sexual intercourse on a ship does not constitute an introduction.' Everyone around stopped talking and the poor sod slunk away with his tail between his legs. Captain almost choked on his gin and tonic trying to stop himself laughing."

"Mmm. Sorry Jenny. What did you say?" Georgina had been mentally re-living her time with Adam Reynolds during dinner, trying to remember everything he'd said and how he looked when he smiled. And why had her heart had missed a beat when his hand accidentally touched hers? And *had* it been accidental?

Realizing Georgina was not listening to her, Jenny yawned noisily. "I'm knackered. I'm off to bed. See you in the morning. Good night, George."

Georgina undressed swiftly. "Jenny, what was Vince doing - er... were you...

"Shagging? No, we were playing snakes and ladders. Christ - grow up, George. Now, shut up, *please.*"

Georgina plumped up her pillow furiously, deciding that was last time she would ask her *anything.* What Jenny did was none of her business and she obviously didn`t want to talk about Vince. She just hoped it wasn't going to be a nightly occurrence, otherwise she'd probably finish up sleeping in the gangway.

And anyway, who was she to question anyone else's morals when she was lying here lusting after Adam Reynolds? She must forget him and try to sleep.

Jenny suddenly sat up in her bunk. "I forgot. How did you go on with the Reynolds bloke. Did he try to have his wicked way with you?"

"Certainly not," replied Georgina primly. "In fact, he was a perfect gentleman. Jenny - his wife wasn't with us. It was just the two of us."

"Not his wife, that's why, George."

"What do you mean? She's called Reynolds. Eve Reynolds."

"That's 'cos she's his *sister.* Go to sleep. We dock in Madeira tomorrow."
Georgina closed her eyes, a warm glow creeping over her. Her heart was singing. She wasn't tired anymore. A little voice inside her repeated over and over again. "He's not married. He's not married."

Chapter Three

"Wake up, George. We can have breakfast on deck this morning and you'll be able to see the ship docking. The weather's glorious."
Georgina peered out of the porthole, pleased to see a tranquil ocean. Starlight and the seas were obviously at one this morning. They were cruising along at a steady pace. This was how the passengers liked it. The speeding up to around twenty two knots to try and make up the time lost during the storm would come through the night when most of them were asleep.

Georgina gasped with pleasure at the sight of a school of dolphins racing along side, leaping, twisting and turning in the air, smiling their delight at having something to race against. A shoal of flying fish leaping high out of the water, glinted a silvery blue as the sun light caught them.

"Shall we be able to go ashore, Jenny?" She jumped out of bed, anxious to make an early start and longing to walk on dry land for a few hours.
"I'm sure if I don't, I'll start to quack."
Jenny laughed at Georgina's reference to the 'duck walk', their way of moving around the ship. To maintain a balance, they walked splay-footed which, although not over attractive, did stop many accidents.

"Let me tell you, George, before long you'll be walking like that permanently, whether on dry land or at sea. It's a habit that`s difficult to get out of. Don't know yet if we'll be allowed ashore. There's a staff meeting at ten. Some of us will have to stay, that's for sure."

"Why?" asked Georgina. "Surely we won't be needed. Won't all the passengers be going ashore?"

"If only," moaned Jenny. "No, the seasoned travellers - and there are many - will stay on board. They've seen it all before. They'll be looking for entertainment. Bingo, gambling, games competitions, coffee, ice cream and most important, the complaints. 'Cos when people are together in a confined area, they become petty. Little things become mountainous. I've seen grown men ready to fight over the result of a quoits game. Unfortunately, we're there to take the brunt of it. And most of the restaurant staff have to work, of course. Lots of passengers, even if they go ashore come back to the ship for meals. Paid for them you see. No point paying again for something probably not as good as they'll get on board. And, the company would rather they ate on board cos they know then what they're eating. Food poisoning, you see. Pick it up ashore and then blame the ship's catering."

Georgina gazed at her in admiration. "You're not just a pretty face, are you Jenny? You really know this business inside out."

"Got to, George, to survive. You'll be OK kid. Just chill out a bit. Keep your mouth shut and your eyes and ears open."

"Jenny..."

Jenny sighed. "*Now* what?"

"Sorry. It's just that I don't want to put my foot in it. You know at the first staff meeting, you asked Pete how Mandy was. Is she his wife?"

"No," replied Jenny slowly." "Mandy's his daughter. Pete married a friend of mine. Sylvie. A dancer. On this ship, actually. They were really happy. Then Mandy was born. Sylvie didn't want her. Pete wanted her to stay at home and look after the child, but she wouldn't do it. Wanted her career, you see. Said she'd worked too hard to give it all up. And - she couldn't give up cruising. It's a strange sort of life, Georgina. Insular. A little world of our own. Once you've experienced it, it's almost impossible to settle down to life ashore. Sylvie tried, but after three months she left Mandy with her mother and joined another cruise ship. Met a millionaire - well she says he is... , but he wouldn't take Mandy." Jenny shrugged her shoulders. "Can't blame him really, can you? What bloke wants another fella's sprog. Anyway, it was all academic 'cos Pete wouldn't have let her go. Mandy, I mean. He adores her and he gets on well with Sylvie's mum, so he's able to see Mandy whenever he wants. So be warned, George. Keep your legs shut as well as your mouth, unless of course, you know what you're doing." Jenny laughed. "Like what I do. *Don't* get pregnant. The company'll send you home anyway if you do. Now - get *up.*"

Georgina squealed as Jenny squeezed a sponge filled with cold water over her face.

The two girls joined the queue for breakfast on deck. This was the first time it had been possible to dine outdoors and most were taking advantage of the sunshine, even though it was a little weak so early in the morning.

"Do we sit with the passengers?" asked Georgina.

Jenny grimaced. "Not if we can help it. Not at this time in the morning. See enough of them the rest of the day. There's Dave. Let's share his table."

"Hi, girls. Did you know we have to rehearse today? No going ashore for any dancers."

"*Shit.*" Jenny spoke vehemently. "I wanted to buy a couple of bottles of

Madeira. Ah well, I'll ask Vince to get them for me."

"Oh no, Jenny, you're not bonking *him* again, are you?" Dave frowned at her. "I thought you said you were going to keep away from officers this trip."
Jenny tapped her nose and stuck out her tongue.

Dave continued, unperturbed. "You should give him the elbow, Jen. Have you seen the entertainment list? Who do you think's coming on at Barbados?"

Jenny put the piece of toast she been about to eat back on the plate. "He's *not,* is he? Oh, it's not *Jock*, is it? Oh Dave*, thanks*. I didn't know."
Georgina smiled as she watched Jenny. Her face positively glowed.

"Er... someone you know, is it Jenny?" she inquired, feigning innocence.

"Someone I *know?* He is the love of my life. I'd *die* for him."

Dave caught Georgina's eye and winked. "Shall I tell him about Vince?"

"You do, Dave and I'll have your balls off."

"Did you know we can't go ashore?"

They were joined by Anna, carrying a dish of melon and strawberries. Dark haired and beautifully tanned, dressed in regulation navy blue skirt and white shirt, her slim dancer's hips swaying provocatively as she walked, she was aware that she invoked the envy of most of the female passengers and attracted the attention of their husbands. One old man tried to pat her bottom as she passed, but she adroitly avoided him and glared balefully at him till he looked away, embarrassed.

"It's not bloody good enough." She pouted prettily. "If everyone came to rehearsals on *time,*" she paused, "we'd probably have the day off."

Georgina blushed, recognising the innuendo. She opened her mouth to respond apologetically, but before she could speak, Jenny, leaning back languidly in her chair and in deceptively honeyed tones said, "Piss off, smarty pants."

To Georgina's amazement, Anna left without retaliating.

"Don`t give her any more opportunities to get at you, George. She can be vicious when she wants. See you at the meeting."

Dave sighed and shook his head as he and Georgina watched Jenny's retreating figure. "She's a worry."

"She's a pet," retorted Georgina.

"She's a fool. Do you want more coffee?"

"No - no thanks. Why did you say that, Dave?"

"Thought you might be thirsty."

Georgina chuckled. "Idiot. You know what I mean. Why is Jenny a fool?"

"Because, my dear," he adopted a theatrical voice, "like Othello, she loves, not wisely, but too well." Dave looked around him. "Do you see the bleached blonde over there?"
Georgina followed his gaze discreetly and nodded.
"She's the ships nympho. She's sailed on the last ten cruises, always on this ship. Anything in pants will do. The lads are all terrified of her. Once she gets her claws in, she doesn't let go. Watch how she works."
Georgina shifted her chair slightly to have a better view of the woman. Aged about forty and dressed in the briefest of bikinis, in spite of a cool breeze blowing across the Atlantic. Not bad looking, but access to unlimited food appeared to have taken its toll and the surplus flesh hanging over and out of the skimpy apparel seemed to Georgina destined to put off even the most undiscriminating male.
Although the dining area was extremely busy, the woman had placed a book on each of the three empty chairs at her table. Georgina watched with interest as an attractive young officer appeared, carrying a breakfast tray, obviously searching for an empty table. He caught sight of the scantily dressed female and made a determined detour away from her, but she immediately stood up and followed him and with a nimbleness that belied her bulky form, took the tray from him.
"Over here, darling. I've saved a place for you."
And as the officer meekly followed her she looked around, triumphantly.
Dave gave a sharp, humourless laugh. "See what I mean. She does it all the time. She thinks she's one of us. And she's such a regular traveller, she has the Captain's ear, so woe betide anyone who upsets her."
Georgina looked puzzled."So - is it common knowledge? Does she actually - I mean - does she have officers - in her cabin? I thought Pete said that fraternising was not allowed?"
"Pete has no jurisdiction over officers, George. Only over us. The officer's are the Captain's department. We're not supposed to have a close relationship with passengers. However, this one seems to have rules made for her. And she's generous, you see. In the bar. Late at night, she buys drinks for the lads. Well, there're not going to look a gift horse in the mouth. And when they've had a few drinks - well - three months is a long time at sea. And she's always available."
"But Dave, she's not exactly - attractive, is she?"
Dave smiled at her, touching her cheek tenderly. "You're a bit of a child,

aren't you Georgina? I don't think you're aware of the wicked ways of men" he laughed teasingly. "I said, we're on a ship, girl. Fella's don't care whether a woman's fat, thin, tall, small, ugly, lovely. In fact, some of them don't even care if it's a woman or another bloke. Come on. We'd better not be late for Pete's meeting. And - we have lifeboat drill when the passengers that are going ashore have gone. Hey, watch out. The Reynolds woman's coming over here."

Eve Reynolds stopped and glared at them. "Have you nothing better to do than sit here gossiping. Clear this table at once. There are passengers looking for somewhere to sit."

Georgina looked around. There were plenty of empty tables, but she stood up immediately and smiled sweetly. "Certainly madam. At once, madam." The woman looked at her suspiciously and opened her mouth to reply but Georgina had turned and walked away from her. She was learning the game. See all, hear all, say nothing.

She walked hurriedly to catch up with Dave and almost collided with a couple. "I'm so sorry," she gasped.

A now familiar voice replied icily. "Do watch where you're going, girl." It was Adam Reynolds. Draped on his arm was a tall, deeply-tanned blonde, beautifully dressed in a white shirt and well-tailored shorts.

"There's a table here, Adam darling." Her voice was possesive, making it clear to Georgina that she was dismissed.

Georgina sighed as she walked away. They belonged to another world. A world in which she had no part. But that did not stop her from being consumed with jealousy at the sight of them so close together. And, with a myriad of thoughts chasing through her mind, Georgina realized that she loved him.

Midnight. Starlight was being made ready to leave Madeira. Georgina leaned on the rail, watching with interest the activities that are involved when a great liner is due to sail. Tiny boats thronged around her, the light from a silvery moon catching them in its beam. Although the main decks were thronged with passengers awaiting the vessels departure, the stern deck was, apart from Georgina, deserted. Georgina stared down into the black waters of the Atlantic, its waves lapping the side of the ship as if playfully saying goodbye. Georgina shivered as a cool wind swept across the deck.

"It's fascinating, isn't it?"

The familiar voice sent a tingling tremor down her spine. Without turning, she spoke softly. "Why did you let me make a fool of myself? Why didn't you tell me that she's your sister?"

Adam replied in equally soft tones. "Would it have made any difference, Georgina? You wanted me regardless of whether I was married or not."

Deep indignation rose within her, subsiding immediately as she realised that he was right. She did want him. Desperately. She shivered again, this time not from the cold, but from a rising passion that she resignedly accepted. As she turned towards him, he removed his jacket and draped it round her shoulders, pulling her close to him. She stood on her tiptoes and lifted her face up to him, ready to receive his kisses but he pushed her back roughly, saying brusquely "You can return the jacket tomorrow. Don't stay out too long, you might catch cold. Goodnight, Georgina."

He turned and strode away from her without a backward glance.

Georgina bounced down the gangway to her cabin, praying that Jenny would not be entertaining tonight. With relief, she saw that the waste bucket wasn't outside, giving its warning message not to enter. The cabin was empty and Georgina undressed quickly and climbed into her bunk pounding her pillow angrily. How dare he treat her so cruelly. She hated him. But, as usual, her anger soon subsided and she began to laugh. What a fool she must have looked, standing on tiptoe waiting to be kissed. Her vivid imagination clicked into gear and she comforted herself with the thought that one of these days she might be able to reciprocate. And she fell asleep, devising deliciously devilish and delightful schemes that would make Adam Reynolds look and feel stupid.

Georgina awoke early the next morning and lay quietly stretched out in her bunk bed, not wanting to disturb Jenny, who was still sleeping. The ship was rolling quite heavily again, but Georgina was sure she had found her sea-legs and would have no more problems with the undulating movement. She was feeling completely at ease now, feeling confident in her new job and looking forward to the seven days of what the experienced passengers called real cruising. No ports of call, which some of them considered only interfered with life at sea. And Georgina was making a big effort to learn the naval jargon. She'd learned the difference between port side and starboard, bow and stern and that the rail at the stern was the taffrall, where she had been leaning when Adam had approached her. She sighed deeply. "I must put him out of my mind now," she commanded herself. "Jenny's right. His sort are not for the likes of me."

The rehearsals for the show which was to take place that evening had gone well and the choreographer had either forgotten her outburst or had decided to be magnanimous and forgive her. In fact, he had held her up as an example of how a disciplined dancer should be rehearsing, dancing precisely, without exuding too much energy thus saving her verve and enthusiasm for the show.

Anna, generally accepted as the star performer, could barely contain her envy, recognising at once that Georgina was good, with an ability to learn quickly. The show was to take place in the form of excerpts from one of the London shows she had performed in, so she knew all the songs and found the dance routines easy.

The steward knocked lightly on the door, enough to rouse Jenny from her slumbers. Georgina jumped out of bed and opened the cabin door, taking the tray from the smiling, young Indian. Jenny stretched her arms above her head and then snuggled back under the duvet.

"Only seven days sailing to Barbados George, and then I'll see my love."

Georgina burst out laughing. "You sound like a romantic novel."

"It is romantic. I *adore* him. Can't wait to see him."

"Hm. Jenny, was I imagining things when I saw a certain young officer leaving our cabin the other night?"

"That's got nothing to do with it," responded Jenny, airily. "And anyway, what's that dinner jacket doing here. You crafty *cow. You've* had a bloke in here! You said you were off men. Don't tell me you've fallen for some one on the ship." Jenny was curious now and wasn't going to let go. "Come on. Do tell. I'd tell you. Who is it? Are you madly in love?"

Georgina remained silent. She musn't fall in love with anyone. But she desperately needed someone to speak to. To confide in. Georgina hated living a lie.

"Jenny..., I... if I tell you something, nothing to do with the jacket, will you promise not to tell anyone else?"

"Cross my heart and hope to die. Come on. Spill it."

But caution once again overruled and Georgina could not reveal her secret. "Nothing. It's nothing - really."

"Suit yourself," retorted Jenny, cheerily. "You can have the first shower. Take your time. I'm going to stay here and dream. Just tell me who the jacket belongs to first, though."

Georgina hesitated for a second. "It - belongs to Adam - Mr Reynolds. He loaned it to me last night. He - thought I was cold."

"I would have thought he was capable of keeping any woman warm," laughed Jenny, wickedly, then shrieked loudly as Georgina pulled the duvet away from her and tickled her feet. There was a loud banging from the cabin next door, followed by a torrent of abusive language. The two girls put their hands over their mouths to stifle their giggles and Jenny motioned Georgina to take her shower.

She'd returned Adam's jacket via one of the stewards, fastening a note to it thanking him. "I've made a decision," she told herself. Never again would she allow her emotions to run away with her as far as Adam Reynolds was concerned.

"He'll never get the chance to make a fool of me again."

Today, after her coffee duty, Georgina had a little free time and decided that she would spend it doing a few turns round the deck. The wind was strong and she had to battle her way around the starboard side of the ship. It was, in fact, much wilder than she had expected and she had left her long hair loose. It lashed her face as she struggled, head down, to reach a calmer part of the ship. The vessel suddenly pitched forward and Georgina cried out as she slipped on the wet deck. She felt an arm reach out and grab her. Without looking, she knew it was Adam. She clung to him tightly, knowing that she was small enough to have slipped through the rails of the ship.

"You little fool. What are you doing outside? You could have gone overboard. Don't you know the Atlantic is completely unpredictable." His voice was rough and she began to cry. He gently smoothed her dark, wild hair away from her face. Placing his hand under her chin, he lifted her head and kissed her. Carefully at first and then with growing intensity. Georgina's firmly made resolutions dissolved and she responded to his embraces with equal passion. Rain started to fall heavily and the ship pitched forward again, the sea spraying the pair of them as they kissed. Oblivious now to the weather, Georgina pressed closer to him, her desire to be near him becoming almost unbearable.

"I love you. I want you, Adam."

He released her abruptly and she stumbled, almost falling again.

"You'd better go in."

Taking her arm, he propelled her to a door which would take her inside and quickly turned away from her. She watched him striding along the deck, his hair looking as black as her own as the rain poured down on him.

Slowly, Georgina made her way to her cabin to shower and change. Still feeling the warmth and passion of his lips, she didn't know whether to be happy or sad. What she did know was that she couldn't resist him. She loved him. She loved him so much it hurt. But would he ever love her. When he knew - if he ever knew. But she couldn't tell him. Not yet. Perhaps not ever. She'd probably never see him again after this trip. But the thought of never seeing him again filled her with despair. Should she grab what little happiness she could now?

There were more rehearsals that afternoon. Georgina was beginning to have a deep respect for the choreographer. He was a perfectionist and she appreciated that. She'd always enjoyed the discipline required to be a good performer and as the rehearsal commenced, she lost herself in the rigours of the song and dance routines and it was only when they were directed to take a break, she realised that Eve Reynolds was sitting in the theatre. As she left the stage, the woman beckoned her over.

"What do you think you're playing at, girl?"

Georgina stood before her in silence. Whatever it was she was supposed to have done, she had no intention of allowing this woman to get under her skin.

"Did you hear what I said?"

Quietly, choosing her words carefully, Georgina replied. "Yes. I heard you, madam. But I'm afraid I don't know what you're talking about." She heard a giggle from Anna and she knew that the rest of the team were watching and listening.

"You've set your cap at my brother," she said, raising her voice to almost a shriek. "What were you doing with his jacket? Ah *yes,*" as Georgina registered some surprise. "It was returned to my cabin in error. I won't have it, do you hear? Just watch your step, my girl or you're out."

She turned sharply and left the theatre, leaving Georgina standing silently with her back to the stage.

"Don't let her upset you, George." Dave came up quietly behind her.

"I don't seem to be able to do anything right, do I, Dave?" Her lips quivered and he leaned forward and kissed them.

"Come on, let's have a coffee. Back in ten folks."

As they left, Georgina heard Anna remark loudly, "She'll be trouble all the way that one and we'll all suffer."

Chapter Four

Seven days continuous sailing was bliss for most passengers, but for the entertainment team it meant hours of continuous work. An early breakfast was about the only time they had to themselves and they guarded this period jealously. The weather was now temperate enough for increasingly frustrated active passengers to start playing their deck games although not yet consistently warm enough for the personnel to be given permission to wear 'tropical whites'.

There were many competitions taking place and these had to be supervised and monitored by 'Pete's people' as they called themselves. When the sun shone brilliantly, there was much vying for these duties, but many moans were heard on the days when the chilly Atlantic breezes swept across the open decks.

It was on such a day that quoits competition duty fell to Georgina. Dave had promised to guide her through the initial stages and once she had command of the game and understood the rules, he would leave her to it.

"You must get it right, Georgina. These people know the rules often better than we do and although your word is final, woe betide you if they think you're favouring someone. Right, if you've finished breakfast we'll go to the games deck and I'll show you the ropes."

"The idea, George, is to take three of these rope rings and throw them, one at a time of course, as near as possible to the marked circle at the other end of the deck. The ring nearest to the centre is the winner."

Dave was a good player and an excellent teacher and Georgina was soon able to hold her own with him, although she quickly discovered there was much more to the game than had first appeared.

"You'll be OK, George so long as you remember to be firm. You're in charge. You're the umpire and your word must be final. Don't dither. Make your decision and stick to it. There are some crafty players around and they'll cheat like mad, given half a chance. It's incredible really. The prizes we give are the kind of things that the type of people on here wouldn`t normally give house room to. And yet, once they're involved in this game, the prizes become the most coveted merchandise in the world. Do you know, on our last trip, a husband and wife playing against each other had such a row, he packed his bags and flew back home when we docked at the next port. The wife was devastated, poor bitch.Then she met someone else and I understand she never went home again."

"Georgina laughed. "I don't believe you, Dave. You're making it up."

"S'true. You look cold. You OK?"

Georgina shivered as a particularly strong gust of wind blew, whipping the already rough sea across the deserted deck.

"Let me warm you up a bit, darling." Before she could move away, he was kissing her.

Taken completely by surprise, Georgina remained motionless in his arms and his embraces became more demanding.

Georgina, recovering her senses pushed him away. "No - please Dave. I'm sorry, but - no."

A movement on the upper deck, overlooking the games deck caught her eye and spinning round quickly, she saw Adam Reynolds turn and walk away.

"Two days to wait, George. Two days and then - Barbados and my Jock." The two girls were taking a welcome break before rehearsals started for that night`s show. It was warm enough to wear bikinis and they had skipped lunch so that they could use the deck-loungers which were normally reserved for passengers.

"How long have you known him, Jenny?"

"He's been on the last two world cruises. Comes on for a few weeks to do a speciality spot. The audiences love him. And - so do I."

"Jenny - you know what you were saying about Pete and Sylvie? What kind of a future would you and Jock have? I mean, you said yourself it wasn't easy. Would you give up your career?"

"For Jock - yes I would. I'd stay at home and have dozens of babies. To be honest, George, I've no illusions about this life. The company hold out a carrot but - after twenty five, you're a bit of a has been and I'm twenty three and not even an assistant cruise director yet. That's the carrot, you see. I'll bet Robert Barnes told you at your interview that if you kept your nose clean, you'd make it to Pete's job."

Georgina looked thoughtful. "Yes - yes, he did," she said slowly.

"Well, look how many of us there are. Six of us. How many of us do you think will make it? Hey, I`m getting too serious. Don't listen to me, kid. You enjoy the cruise. It's bloody hard work though, isn't it? By the way, what's happened to the Reynolds bloke?"

Georgina didn't reply. She'd only spotted Adam once since he'd seen Dave kissing her. He'd been standing at the bar when she'd walked in late one evening after appearing in a show. Her heart had missed a beat, and her legs turned to jelly as she caught sight of him. Their eyes met for a brief second and she'd risked an enquiring tremulous smile. He'd turned away pointedly, starting an animated conversation with an attractive young woman standing by his side, placing his arm possessively around her waist.

"Well, *have* you seen him? It's incredible, isn't it, how you can go for days on this ship and not see someone. Mebbe he'll ask you to have dinner with him again sometime. Come on. Rehearsal time."

Relieved, Georgina rose to her feet. She didn't want to talk about Adam Reynolds. As far as she was concerned, she didn't care if she never saw him again.

"Georgina, we've a full day off tomorrow in Barbados. Have you anything arranged?"

Dave handed her a drink as they relaxed in the late night bar after a particularly exhausting show, which had involved many strenuous dance routines. His behaviour had been exemplary since she had rebuffed him on the games deck, even calling her Georgina and not George.

"No - no, I haven't, Dave."

She'd been wondering what she should do when the ship docked. This was to be her first time abroad and she was a bit frightened of going on to the island alone. Jenny was obviously going to meet up with her Jock and the rest of the team were Anna's friends. Georgina was learning that life on board ship could be very lonely.

"Would you like to have a day on the beach?" She hesitated. "I promise to behave. Scouts honour."

He held up two fingers and Georgina laughed. "I believe you, Dave. I'd be delighted. Thank you very much. I haven't anyone else to go ashore with - I mean ... oh dear... that sounds terrible. I didn't mean..."

"Christ, Georgina, shut up and stop being so - *nice.* I know what you mean. Let's be mates, shall we?"

Relieved, Georgina leaned forward and kissed him on the cheek. "Mates it is. Dave - is Jenny going to get hurt? With this Jock, I mean."

Dave frowned. "I honestly don't know. I - hate to say this but - well, she does sleep around a bit, you know. And yet, when Jock's on the ship, she's all over him. Can't get enough of him. And I must say he seems fond of her. But he's a dark horse. Good entertainer, but keeps his cards close to his chest.

And - he drinks a bit too much for my liking. Could be married. Who knows. "He shrugged his shoulders. "It's a funny old world on a ship. Not conducive to happy relationships. I wouldn't get married so long as I'm cruising. It's not fair to a girl. You see, being away for such a long stretch, I couldn't say for sure that I'd be faithful."

Georgina smiled at him. "Well, that's honest anyway. Are there lots of affairs going on?"

"Phew, just you wait till we've been at sea a few more weeks. Passengers, crew, staff, they're all at it. We're all so isolated, remember. Female passengers are the worst. They forget life at home after a while. If you keep your eyes open, you'll see how they start to pair off. Then they get bored and it's all change. You've seen our nympho on the deck grabbing the poor sods. Well, watch this. There she is at the bar with the officers. They like to get together this time of night for a bit of a chat amongst themselves, but she stands with them. She won't leave till she finds one to take back to her cabin. And there's the Doc, touching up the Purser. The Doc's pissed of course. As usual. Hope no one dies during the night."

Georgina gasped. "Hey, I never thought about that. What happens if someone dies?"

Dave laughed a hollow laugh. "Doc certifies them and over they go."

"What do you mean?" Georgina asked, fearfully. "Over where?"

"Over the side, idiot. Where else?"

Georgina shuddered. "Oh Dave, that's *awful.*"

"I'm sure it is, but what else can they do?"

"Couldn't they keep them in the deep freeze?"

Dave threw back his head and roared with laughter. "Oh yes. Chef would be over the moon. I think it's time we went to bed, Georgina."

He viewed her quizzically. "Er... you don't think...?"

"Mates *only,*" interjected Georgina, firmly.

"Just testing. OK. Mates only," he agreed with a deep sigh.

As they left the bar, hand in hand, Adam Reynolds entered with a red headed beauty hanging on to his arm.

"See what I mean," whispered Dave. "You can guess whose bed *she'll* finish up in tonight."

"Let's get out of here, please Dave."

Georgina hurried through the door then stopped, as a commanding voice called out to her. "Miss Murphy. Come here at once."

"You go on , Dave," she whispered. "I'll see you tomorrow."
Georgina turned slowly towards Adam Reynolds. The redhead was no where to be seen. Her heart beat wildly as she stood before him, her eyes lowered.

After a long silence, during which she sensed his piercing, hazel eyes exploring her, he spoke. "You will accompany me in Barbados tomorrow."
Georgina lifted her head and as their eyes met for one electrifying second, she knew without any doubt that she loved him.

"I can't." She lowered her head.

"Please, Georgina." His voice became soft, entreating. "I need to talk to you."

"I promised Dave. We're spending the day together. I... I can't let him down."

"And no doubt you'll be spending the night with him too." His voice was bitter and wounding. "Well, Miss Murphy, I'm ordering you. You will accompany *me* tomorrow."

The genes of generations of Murphys' rebelled at the idea of Georgina allowing herself to be dictated to in such a manner. Her Irish spirit of independence rose impetuously to the surface. Drawing herself to her full five foot one and a half, she spoke scathingly, but with as much dignity as she could muster. "I'm so sorry - *sir,* but tomorrow I am off duty and I will spend my free time exactly as I wish and - *sir* - it will not be with *you."*

As Georgina walked away, her indignation subsided. Dave wouldn't have minded. He'd have understood and she could have had a whole day with Adam. And then she remembered Dave's kindness to her. Why should she abandon him just because of a whim of Adam Reynolds He cared nothing for her. He was only playing with her. He needed a bit of company and she was available. Her indignation returned. Well - she wasn't going to be available. And - she must keep on the right side of Eve Reynolds. She was the important one. She was the director, with the power to dismiss her if she felt so inclined. Even though Adam had intervened once on her behalf, Eve Reynolds had made it clear that it would not happen a second time. No, she'd done the right thing.

"Are you in, Jenny?" she called softly, hoping not to disturb her cabin mate. There was no reply and Georgina switched the light on. The cabin was empty.

"I expect she`s still in one of the bars," she thought.

Putting Adam Reynolds completely out of her mind, Georgina undressed, smiling to herself in anticipation of spending the day in Barbados.

"I'm so lucky to be on this world cruise," she told herself. "I musn't do anything to spoil it."

And Dave was a lovely bloke. He would make someone a super husband one day. Georgina sighed. "It won't be me though."

As the 'Starlight' docked, she was greeted by the local populace, who had provided a steel band and a charming dance team. Georgina leaned on the rail of the ship, watching with misty eyes the younger dancers, some of them appearing to be no older than Rosie. She was joined by Dave and Jenny.

"Look at the little ones. How I wish Rosie could see them."

"Who's Rosie?" asked Dave.

"George's sister," responded Jenny. "You should see her picture, Dave. She's a little darling, isn't she, George?"

"Yes, she is. And we love her to bits, mum and I."

"What about your dad, Georgina."

"Dead."

"Are you ready to go ashore, Georgina? Once all the passengers are off, we'll be able to go. Will Jock be here, Jenny?"

"Yes, he arrived yesterday. He'll be coming on board in about an hours time, I'll help him unpack, then we'll probably go into Bridgetown. Off you go, you two. It looks as if the last passenger is away. Have a good day. And George, don't do too much sunbathing. It's going to be very, *very* hot. And Dave - you look after her, do you hear? If you've got the time, George, try to do some shopping. There's a place called Pelican Village. Sells georgeous silver filigree jewellery."

"I don't think so, Jenny. I'm trying not to spend very much."

"Ah well. Shame. Dave, you'll be wanting some rum surely. Jock will be buying as much as he can although he'd rather have whisky. He's a real Scot." Dave caught Georgina's eye and nodded knowingly.

Georgina gasped in disbelief as they approached the beach. For as far as the eye could see, miles and miles of soft, silvery, unspoiled sand leading into azure waters. The beach was deserted, most of the passengers making straight for the shopping areas to purchase the famous Barbadian rum and to take pictures of the statue of Nelson in Bridgetown's Trafalgar Square.

They found themselves a shady spot under a swaying palm tree and Dave spread out a large towel on which he deposited a cool bag.

"What's in the bag, Dave?" inquired Georgina, stripping off her shorts and T-shirt, revealing a one piece swimsuit. She'd been tempted to wear a bikini but had decided against it. To spend a whole day with Dave in what she felt could be regarded as provocative attire would not be fair. He was, after all, an attractive full blooded male. She knew he fancied her like crazy and she'd no intention of spoiling the day by sending out the wrong signals to him. Even so, she appreciated his admiring appraisal of her. Her blue-black hair hung loosely around her smooth shoulders and her dark green swimsuit matched her eyes perfectly. Her skin, not yet tanned, shone ivory white in the morning sunshine.

"I bribed one of the lads in the kitchen to make up a picnic for us. Come on, race you to the sea."

Hand in hand, they ran towards the sea, laughing like children on their first visit to the sea-side. For an hour, they splashed about and swam in the warm, blue sea, allowing the waves to attack them.

"Watch out for sharks, Georgina."

He dived underneath her, grabbing her legs.

Georgina shrieked and made a dash for the shore. Dave followed her closely, shaking the water from his body. She knelt on the towel, rubbing her hair until it was wild and glorious. Dave looked on in admiration.

"You look like a sea nymph. I've never seen hair like yours before, Georgina."

She laughed. "And you've never seen a sea nymph, have you? Yes, I'm lucky with my hair," she admitted. "And it's not a lot of bother. Just does it's own thing, I suppose. But Dave, you should see my..." she stopped abruptly, "my little sister's. Do you have any family, Dave? Any brothers and sisters, I mean?"

He lay back on the towel, folding his arms underneath his head and stretched out his long legs. "Don't know, Georgina. I was... abandoned at birth, as they say. Brought up in a home, thrown out at sixteen, as per the system. That's why I joined the cruise company. It's a home, companionship, some sort of a family, I suppose. There's a lot of life's casualties working on ships. Not that I'm a casualty," he added quickly, and Georgina recognised that he had tremendous pride. "I don't know who my parents were and quite frankly, I don't care. I've never been able to understand these folk who want to find their parents." He shrugged his shoulders. "What's the point? If they didn't want me when I was born, they won't want me now, will they?"

He spoke without bitterness and Georgina realised that here was what her mother would describe as 'a nice lad'. Why on earth couldn't she fall in love with someone like Dave, instead of an arrogant, obnoxious, impossible man such as Adam Reynolds? She thought of Dave's kisses on the games deck. She'd felt nothing. And she thought of Adam's first kiss in the garage. A kiss that had filled her with overwhelming emotion. And the kisses they had shared on a storm battered deck in the middle of the Atlantic Ocean. And she knew that to satisfy her passionate nature, she couldn't settle for anything less.

Dave sat up suddenly and placed his shirt around her shoulders. "Do take care, Georgina. The sun sort of creeps up on you. Jenny'll never forgive me if you go back with sunburn. Are you hungry?"

Without waiting for a reply, he opened the cool box, revealing a delicious assortment of food. Smoked salmon and caviar. Bite sized pieces of chicken, tiny dishes of salads, plump strawberries, succulent pineapple and ripe melon, all cut into manageable portions. He handed to her with a magnificent flourish, a china plate and a pristine, snowy white napkin taken from one of the ship's restaurants and, diving further into the box, produced with a triumphant shout of "De... dum," a bottle of Chablis and two plastic beakers. The sight of the plastic beakers amongst all the other finery produced peals of helpless laughter from Georgina.

"A feast like this deserves the finest cut glass goblets, Dave," she gasped, wiping tears of laughter from her eyes.

Dave stretched out again and gazed up at the clear blue sky. "I'm doing this job so that I can save enough money, Georgina, to be able to buy nothing but the best for the rest of my life. I only wish I could share it with someone like you."

Georgina looked down at him, sadly. "You know nothing about me, Dave. Maybe I'm not what you think I am. And now," she said briskly, "I don't know about you, but I'm *starving*." She suddenly remembered something.

"Dave, there aren't *really* any sharks, are there?"

Dave laughed and sat up. "Just you swim too far out there and you'll soon find out?" "Have you enjoyed the day, Georgina?"

"Oh, Dave, it`s been wonderful. Thank you very much."

"So... what are you going to do for the rest of the evening? You should make the most of your free time. We get very little of it. The ship doesn't sail till midnight. We could go into Bridgetown and have a meal ashore for a change. My treat."

Georgina smiled her thanks. "Save your money Dave, for those crystal wine glasses. No, if you don't mind, I should write some letters and then I'll probably have an early night. Catch up with some sleep. Thanks again for the day. I'll see you at breakfast."

Georgina finished writing the postcards she had bought and took them to the purser's desk, popping them in the box which would shortly be emptied and the contents taken ashore, soon to be winging their way to their recipients.

"Hello, my dear."

Georgina turned to see 'Old Mother Riley' sitting on a large settee. The old lady patted the empty space beside her.

"Come and keep an old lady company for a little while."

Georgina smiled and sat down beside her.

"You didn't get sent home after all, did you?" She leaned towards Georgina and whispered confidentially. "I had a word with Eve Reynolds. Told her not to be such a fool. I've known her many years, you know. She hasn't always been so embittered. Used to be a beautiful woman. Well, I suppose she still is."

"Did she ever marry?" inquired Georgina, eager to know something of the Reynolds.

"She was going to be. Old Mr Reynolds, he was the chairman of the company and she was the apple of his eye. Adam, you see, wasn't interested in shipping. All he was interested in was music. Plays the piano quite beautifully. Have you met Adam? Now Eve, she loved the business. Travelled everywhere with her father. She should have been the boy. Anyway, on one trip, she fell in love with one of the engineers. Old Mr Reynolds was furious. He was quite an old man, you see. One of the old school. Adam and Eve's mother was half his age. Am I boring you, child?"

"Oh no," breathed Georgina. "Do go on, please."

"He forbade her to marry him. Said that if she did, he would cut her off from the business. Well, Eve couldn't bear that. It was her life. She flew back home as soon as the ship docked. Within a few weeks, she realised she was pregnant and sought out her engineer, but he'd left the ship at Sydney, taking one of the dancers with him. She had an abortion and rumour has it she's never looked at another man since. The following year, both old Mr Reynolds and his wife were killed in an air crash. You may have read about it."

Georgina shook her head. "That's all very sad. But - she couldn't have really loved him, could she? The engineer, I mean. If she had, she wouldn't have cared about the money or the business. If I loved someone, I'd move heaven and earth to be with him."

"Have you ever been rich? Really rich. Georgina?" The old lady smiled at her, questioningly.

"No, but..."

"Then, my dear, you wouldn't know what it's like to give it up, would you? It's easy to be idealistic and principled when you don't have anything."

"That sounds very cynical." Georgina's voice expressed her disappointment in her companion.

"It's all this cruising, my dear," Mrs Riley laughed. "Brings out the worst in the human race, I can tell you. Anyway," she patted Georgina's knee, "I'm delighted that you're still with us. Now, what else can I tell you?"

"Adam, Mr Reynolds. Is he - married?" Georgina had realised that she'd been so delighted to learn that Eve was not his wife, it hadn't occurred to her that he may indeed be married to someone else.

"No. He's much younger than Eve. After their parent's death, Eve looked after him. I suppose he became her baby. She frightens off any woman that shows an interest in him. It amuses him and I think he humours her. Mind you, he's a strong enough character to please himself if and when he meets the right woman."

"Mrs Riley, how do you know so much about the Reynolds?"

"Oh, it's common knowledge amongst the cruising fraternity. It's not easy to keep a secret on a ship, so don't tell anyone anything you don't want the whole ship to know, my dear. It'll go through the cabins, into the restaurant, round the kitchens and along the decks, becoming increasingly embellished. Not that you look as if you have anything to hide. You're far too young to have a murky past. Not like your cabin mate. She's a bit of a flibbertigibbet. Ah yes," as Georgina opened her mouth to protest, "I don't miss much."

The old lady rose carefully. "I must go to bed now. I won't wait to watch 'Starlight' sail away. I've seen too may departures to get excited. By the way, that young man Dave's not for you. Read'em like a book. Goodnight, Georgina."

Georgina stayed seated a long time after 'Old Mother Riley' had gone, thinking over what she had said. Not easy to keep a secret, she'd said. And that she didn't look as if *she* had anything to hide. "Oh God," she thought. "If only that were true."

The 'Starlight's' horn sounded its commanding message. The ship was ready to leave. Georgina awoke with a start. She was still curled up on the settee. Wearily, she made her way to the cabin, hoping that no one had seen her. It wouldn't do for a member of the staff to be seen asleep in a public place. She undressed quickly and, skipping her shower, climbed into her bunk and fell into a deep, dreamless sleep.

When she awoke the following morning, the tea tray was already on the dressing table. The steward had been in without disturbing her.

"Hey, Jenny. What's the time?"

There was no reply and Georgina lifted her head cautiously, peering into the top bunk. It hadn't been slept in. For a few seconds she was confused and concerned until she remembered. Jenny's Jock was on board. She smiled as she realised she would probably have the cabin to herself for the next few weeks. Pouring a cup of tea, she slipped back into bed. Both she and Jenny were on coffee duty this morning and later on they were to help passengers make costumes for that evening's fancy dress competition. Georgina leaned back on the pillow and sipped her tea, trying to digest what Mrs. Riley had told her about the Reynolds. If what she'd said was true, and Georgina was inclined to believe her, then perhaps Eve's past was a reason for her bitterness. She began to feel sorry for her. And, what was more important - Adam wasn't married. She closed her eyes and sank into a reverie, where she and Adam were running across the silver sands on the beach, as she and Dave had done yesterday. She snuggled deliciously beneath the duvet, drifting off to sleep again.

The cabin door swung open, waking her with a start, and Jenny burst in.

"Ah, great. Tea. Can I have the first shower, George? Did you and Dave have a good day?"

"Wonderful." Georgina was fully conscious again and remembering what good company Dave had been. "Really great. Did you?"

"Had a better night, darling."

Georgina laughed. "I take it he arrived then."

"George, if I let you in to a secret, you won't tell anyone, will you"?

"No, Jenny. I won't tell anyone."

Jenny undressed quickly and stood naked in front of the mirror, running her hands over her slim body. An area of her neck was beginning to discolour into what was obviously a passionate love bite. She touched it gently with her finger tips, smiling secretly.

"He's asked me to marry him."

Georgina was silent.

"Well," demanded Jenny. "What do you think?"
"I don't know - him, do I Jenny? If you think you'll be happy, then I'm delighted for you. When?"

"Oh, not for ages yet. It's a commitment, though, isn't it? Now - remember, George, keep it quiet. Jock doesn't want anyone to know."

"Why?"

"What do you mean, why?"

"What I said - why? If I was going to be married, I'd want the whole world to know."

Jenny stared at her, coldly. "Well, it's not you is it? This is how it has to be. I wish I hadn't told you. I thought you'd be thrilled for me."

"Oh - I am, Jenny. Honest I am." Georgina put her arms around her and hugged her. "And Jenny, if you want something for your neck, I have some cover-up in my bag. Help yourself."

Jenny looked at her in amusement. "Not likely. There's nothing like the sight of a love bite for turning blokes on."

Georgina burst out laughing. "Jenny, you're incorrigible."

"Do you fancy a swim, George? The pools empty and we've half an hour before coffee duty."

"Oh, that would be wonderful," gasped Georgina. "I'm so hot I can scarcely breath."

Jenny chuckled. "You ain't seen nothun' yet. Wait till we're nearer the equator. Come on, let's go."

They walked quickly towards the pool, meeting Anna on the way.

"Hi. Have you heard the news?"

"Well, if you're itching to tell us, it must be bad," retorted Jenny sarcastically.

Anna looked pointedly at Jenny's neck. "I see the Scotsman's back in town."

"Stop it, you two." Georgina halted the antagonistic interchange between them. "What is it? What's happened?"

"Old Mother Riley's dead."

Georgina stared at her in disbelief. "That's a *terrible* thing to say, Anna. How could you joke about a thing like that?"

"When did it happen, Anna?" asked Jenny quietly

Georgina stared from one to the other in dismay.

"During the night. Heart attack. Buried her at six."

Georgina leaned heavily against the wall. She felt sick.

"But - I was speaking to her late last night. She was alright then. Anna, are you sure?"

Anna gave a short laugh. "Well, if I'm not, they chucked her in alive. Course I'm sure, idiot. See you at the fancy dress." Georgina watched in dismay as she walked away, her slender hips swaying provocatively as she passed a male passenger.

Georgina shuddered. "*Surely* Jenny, they'll cancel the fancy dress?"

Jenny shrugged her shoulders. "Why should they? Here, don't you tell any passengers. They'll find out, but not from us. Understand? Nothing, but *nothing* interferes with the *en-ter-tain-ment*." She dragged the word out, bitterly. "We're here to please. To amuse. Passengers don't want to know about anything unpleasant. You'll see that when you accompany a coach on the tours ashore. They only want to see the *nice* places in a country. The slums make them feel uncomfortable, you see. Spoils their holiday. Let's get changed and into that pool before it's too crowded."

"I can't," said Georgina tearfully.

"You can. And you *will*" replied Jenny, firmly. "Listen - you'll get used to it. It happens all the time. There are lots of old people on cruises. Some of them die. It's inevitable. They'd die if they were at home. You'll find that hardly anyone will mention it. Not their business, see. It's not yours either." Jenny glanced at her watch. "We've fifteen minutes left. Race you."

"I'll take the port side if you like," whispered Jenny. "The Glums are there. I know you don't feel like speaking much this morning."

"No - no, I'm OK Jenny. It's my turn to have them. Listen, what's their real name? I'm terrified I call her Mrs Glum."

Jenny didn't answer immediately. She looked at Georgina with a serious expression on her face. "It's - Mr and Mrs Moody."

Georgina began to laugh. She laughed untill the tears trickled down her face. But her tears were a mixture of amusement and sorrow. Sorrow for a dear old lady who had been kind to her.

"That's my girl. But, steady on now. Here's Pete."

"Hi, girls. Glad to see you're both in fine fettle. Georgina, I've been asked to give you this?" He handed a letter to her.

"Who's it from" she asked, puzzled.

"God," laughed Pete. "Typical female. Open the bloody thing and find out. Here's the coffee. Off you go and keep the punters happy."

He walked away, nodding and smiling to everyone, weaving in and out of the table, expertly avoiding being waylaid.

Georgina frowned. "I hate that word, punters. I feel as if we're - well... using them."

Jenny laughed. "We are. Would you willingly spend the next ten minutes chatting to the Glums if you had a choice?"

Georgina hesitated. "No - no I don't suppose I would."

"Course you wouldn't. None of us would. You're being over sensitive George, but you're in danger of sounding bloody sanctimonious. Harden up. Are you going to open that letter?"

Georgina pushed it in her pocket. "I'll look at it later. Glums - here I come."

An hour later, Georgina, exhausted after an inordinate session with the Moodys, as she was now determined to call them, flopped on to a lounger by the side of the pool. She'd been determined to try to find some common ground with the couple, to cheer them up a bit, perhaps. She soon realised however that the Moodys were professional moaners and no matter how hard she tried, she could not divert them from their belief that the full compliment of crew and staff of the 'Starlight' were out to defraud them and that they were lazy, incompetent and ignorant. That they were all fornicators from the deputy Captain down. The Captain, it seemed, was excluded, he having his wife travelling with him. Eventually, Georgina learned to do what all 'Pete's people' did. She turned off and hoped that she nodded, shook her head and tut-tutted in the right places.

The letter was burning a hole in her pocket. Who would be writing to her? She hardly knew anyone yet. Georgina took it out, staring at the outside, as if the typewritten name, Miss G Murphy, could reveal the identity of the writer. Becoming impatient with herself, she carefully opened the envelope and slowly extracted the letter, glancing at the bottom first. Yes - *yes*. Her heart sang. She'd known deep down it would be from him. It was signed - Adam. As she read it, the now familiar tingling began in her spine and her hands shook.

"Irish," it began. "As you appear to be in great demand, may I book you for the day to accompany me when we reach Los Angeles? This is some distance away but please Georgina, will you write it in your diary?"

The tone of the letter was so different to his usual manner, Georgina was sure he was trying to make amends for his earlier rudeness. She put the letter to her lips.

"I will, my darling. Oh, a whole day together. Just the two of us."

Resisting an urge to run, she made her way to the Purser's desk, picked up a sheet of note paper and wrote in giant letters, 'YES, YES, YES. Georgina.' Placing it in an envelope, she addressed it to ADAM REYNOLDS, and handed it to the girl behind the desk.

"Would you have that put in Mr Adam Reynold's cabin, please?"

"Certainly." The girl smiled beyond her. "Hello, Jock. Good to see you back again. How long are you on for this time?"

"Till after Burn's night. Good to see you, too."

Georgina froze. She knew that voice. Oh please God, don't let it be him. Turning around slowly, Georgina found herself face to face with her ex-lover, Hugh Campbell.

"Georgina. Good Lord. What are you doing here?"

Her head was spinning. Her throat and lips dry. She tried to speak, but no sound emerged.

"Let's get out of here."

Taking hold of her arm, he led her down the staircase and along the gangway.

"Where are we going?" Georgina didn't recognise her own voice.

"To my cabin."

She stopped sharply and gasped. "N... no. I can't. I musn't."

"Georgina," he snapped impatiently. "I'm not going to *rape* you. We must talk. Are you on holiday?"

Stopping in front of a cabin, he took out a key and opened the door. "Get in, Georgina."

The heavy cabin door swung shut behind her and she instinctively turned to go out again.

"Stop it, you litle fool. I'm not going to hurt you. I've changed Georgina. Let me look at you." He drew in his breath, sharply. "Jesus. You're lovely."

"Don't, Hugh. Please - don't."

"Georgina - what about the baby? Was it a boy or a girl. Why didn't you let me know what was happening? Why did you just disappear?"

"You could have found me, Hugh if you'd really wanted. You didn't want the baby. Remember. You wanted me to have an abortion and you knew I couldn't. You knew I was a Catholic. You hit me, Hugh. You got drunk and you hit me. I could never marry a man who would resort to violence. I couldn't have married you right then anyway. I was only fifteen. You can't hold your drink, Hugh. I - miscarried. There is no baby. Thats what you wanted, wasn't it? After, I went back to the West End."

"Georgina, you didn't want me to find you. You made that perfectly clear." He was right, of course, thought Georgina. She'd left him under no illusions that she didn't ever want to see him again.
"I - thought it was only fair, Hugh. Give you a chance to get on with your life. Meet someone else. And you have, haven't you? You've met Jenny. You're her Jock, aren't you?"
He gazed at her in amazement. "How do you know Jenny?"
She smiled at him, wanly. "I'm not on holiday, Hugh. I work on the ship. Jenny's my cabin mate."
She sat down despairingly on a chair. "Hugh - don't tell Jenny that I - know you. Please. Let's keep it a secret. She'd be so upset. Please, Hugh. I couldn't bear that."
Raising her eyes to his, she gazed at him unwaveringly. "You owe me nothing Hugh and I certainly don't owe *you* anything. We were just - ships that pass in the night."
He took hold of her hands. "I'm sorry about the baby. I'm sorry I hit you. I did love you, Georgina."
"I know," she whispered. "And I once thought I loved you. Will you do as I ask, Hugh? Pretend we're strangers. I'm very fond of Jenny. She's helped me so much. And - she told me that you'd asked her to marry you."
"I asked her not to tell anyone."
"She's only told me, Hugh and I won't tell anyone. Why has it got to be a secret?"
He hesitated before replying. "I won't do anything to hurt her, Georgina. You can be sure of that."
"You'd better not hurt her, Hugh. Don't you ever lay a finger on her and - keep of the whisky, Hugh. I'd better go." Georgina stood up and smiled sadly at him. "It's a small world, isn't it?"
"Sure is." He laughed nervously. "I'll - look forward to meeting you, Georgina. Officially, I mean."
Georgina went back to her cabin, thankful that Jenny was not in. She stood and looked around her. What was she to do? She'd been so happy in this job. Now she wanted to hide herself away. Away from Jenny, away from Hugh, away from prying eyes. But she was on a ship. In the middle of the ocean, from which there was no escape. She began to cry, quietly at first and then she threw herself on to the bunk, her body racked with heart-rending sobs. Crying as though her heart was breaking. She'd taken this job with such

enthusiasm and it was all going pear shaped. Firstly, she lied at her interview. Now she was going to be lying to Jenny and everyone. And asking Hugh to lie too. She felt she was sinking deeper and deeper into the mire.What a catastrophic coincidence that Hugh should be working on this ship. And that Jenny should be her cabin-mate. Her tears gradually subsided and she sat up, reaching out for Rosie's picture and kissed it gently.

"I won't let you down, sweetheart. Nor you, mum. I promise I'll stick it out come what may. You'll both be proud of me."

"Are you OK Georgina? You don't look very well"

The two girls were relaxing in their cabin after a particularly gruelling afternoon.

"I'm OK, Jenny. It's been a bit of a hard day, what with the fancy dress and old Mrs Riley and everything." Georgina laughed, humourlessly. "You were right about the company though. They do extract every ounce of energy from us, don't they? I'm not quite used to it yet."

"George, Jock will be the compere at the show tonight. Will you join us in the bar afterwards? I want you to meet him."

Georgina groaned inwardly. She couldn't face seeing Hugh again so soon.

"Jenny - I can't" she began hesitantly.

"Please George. You *must* meet him. To tell me what you think."

"Jenny - if you're absolutely sure about him, you shouldn't care what anyone else thinks. I'll meet him tomorrow."

Georgina was determined not to see him tonight. It was too soon. She needed time to think. "Jenny, I'm going to ask Pete to let me have the night off. I know it's not the thing to do, but I really don't think I can dance tonight."

Jenny looked doubtful. "You can try, but he won't like it. Slip along to his office. He should be in at this time."

"I don't usually let anyone skip a show, Georgina, unless there's a *very* good reason." Pete frowned. "It's not fair to the others, you see."

"I know that, Pete. I wouldn't ask if I wasn't desperate. I'm not being lazy. It's - a bit personal. I promise I'll never ask again."

He gazed at her speculatively. "Are you OK, Georgina? Would you like a coffee?"

He went over to a coffee maker and Georgina took the opportunity to look around her. Pete's cabin was much bigger than her shared one. There was a bed instead of the usual bunks and a settee, a couple of easy chairs and a large desk.

"Nice cabin," she commented.

He stared around. "Yes, I suppose it is. I spend most of my life here, Georgina."

She recalled what Jenny had told her about his wife and his daughter, Mandy.

"I'm sorry, Pete. I didn't mean to be nosy."

He handed her a cup of coffee. "You're not. Now, do you like life at sea, Georgina?"

"Thank you. Yes - I think I do."

"Only think. You're not sure yet? I don't have much time to chat, but we do like to keep a happy team. I know it's hard work, but well - that's what we're all here for, isn't it? And, the rewards are good. Finish your coffee, Georgina. Go and sort out whatever it is you have to sort out. And, yes, take the night off. You must have caught me in a good mood. Make the most of it. It doesn't happen often."

Georgina stood up and turned to leave.

"Oh, I almost forgot, Georgina. Mr and Miss Reynolds are holding a cocktail party in their cabin tomorrow evening. They especially asked for you to be there."

"Me," she gasped. "At a cocktail party?"

Pete laughed. "Not as a guest, you fool. To help serve the drinks. Hand out canapes and pickles. You know, the usual thing."

"But why, Pete? Why me? Is Jenny to be there? Who - who asked for me. Was it *Miss* Reynolds?"

Pete frowned. "Ours is not to reason why. Does it matter who asked for you?"

"Yes, yes - as it happens it does. Pete, is it usual for one of your people to be asked to serve at a cocktail party? Is that not a job for a waitress or a steward?"

Pete looked at her coldly. "Get this into your head, Georgina. It doesn't matter whose job it is. Don't get too high and mighty. We're all here to serve. Passengers request - demand - and we jump. And when a director is involved - we move our arses pretty quick if we want to keep our job. Now, off you go before I change my mind about your night off."

Subdued and suitably chastised, Georgina opened the cabin door.

"George," Pete smiled at her, kindly now. "It was Adam who asked for you. Adam Reynolds. Not a director, I know, but as near as damn it."

Jenny was fast asleep when Georgina returned to their cabin. She sat on the edge of her bunk trying to suppress the rage that was rising inside her. How *dare* Adam Reynolds treat her so. She knew what his little game was. He was determined to keep her in her place. To remind her that she was a paid servant of the company. That she must remain servile whilst he and his fine friends nibbled at their stupid canapes and drank their stupid drinks. He'd tricked her into thinking that his attitude towards her had changed. He'd probably produce her note. That silly, eager schoolgirlish reply and they'd all have a good laugh. *She* would be the evening's entertainment. Unable to contain herself any longer, she threw herself full length on her bunk, pummelling the pillows. And for a girl brought up in a household that had frowned on the use of bad language of any kind, she shocked herself at the amount of blasphemous abuse she was able to hurl at her tormentor. Finally exhausted, she finished her outburst on a lighter note.

"I hate him. I'll probably *kill* him. Yes, that's what I'll do. I'll push him over the side. And wave him goodbye. And the sharks will gobble him up, starting with his bollocks."

Jenny's amused face appeared over the side of the bunk. "That's a bit drastic, isn't it? Poor Pete. Wouldn't he let you have the night off?" she asked innocently. "I did warn you."

Georgina began to laugh ruefully at her own absurdity. "No, it's not Pete, Jenny. It's that Reynolds. That hateful, horrible - male - *man.*"

Jenny smiled at the venom in Georgina's voice.

"Methinks that the lady hateth too much."

"That's a misquote."

"I know, but it's true, isn't it. You fancy him, don't you? Go on George. Admit it."

Georgina turned over onto her back and closed her eyes. "Yes. I love him, Jenny," she admitted softly. "I love him so much I could die. I've never felt like this before. Not even..."

"Not even - what?" asked Jenny, her curiosity aroused now. "Have you been in love before, George? Come on, tell Aunty Jen. Do you have a dark and secret past?"

"Don't tease, Jenny, I really don't want to talk about it."

Jenny stared at Georgina's sticken face. "Sorry, love. I won't ask you anymore. But whatever's happened - forget it. The past's dead."

Georgina opened her eyes and gazed at the picture of Rosie. "No, it's not, Jenny. My past is very much alive, thank God."

Jenny followed Georgina's gaze and comprehension slowly dawned on her.
"She's not your sister, is she? Rosie's yours. She's your child. Why didn't you *say.* Do you know who the father is, Georgina?"

Georgina sat up sharply. "Jenny - Jenny, listen to me."

Jenny, silenced by the urgency in Georgina's voice, jumped down from her bunk and sat beside her.

"No one must know. Do you understand? If anyone on this ship finds out, I shall know where it came from and I'll never forgive you. *Never.*" Georgina's voice began to rise hysterically.

"Here, steady on, girl. We're mates, aren't we? I won't tell. But - what's the big deal? So you've got a kid. It's not a hanging matter, is it?"

"Promise." Georgina looked at Jenny, pleadingly.

"I promise. Georgina, if ever you want to talk about it, I'm here." She picked up the photograph. "She's a doll. A credit to you. You shouldn't be hiding her. You should be proud of her. I'll bet there's some bloke out there doesn't know what he's missing. I must shower ready for the show. *Some* of us have to work. We're not all teacher's pet."

But Georgina was in no mood for banter and after Jenny had left, she closed her eyes and tried to make sense of what she had said. She'd lied to Hugh when she told him she'd mis-carried so why on earth had she told Jenny the truth? She felt possessed, urged on by some suicidal force that was beyond her control. And these two people, Jenny and Hugh now held two pieces of the jig-saw that could - would - result in the ending of her contract on this trip. Robert Barnes would not forgive her for lying and he would be quite within his rights to dismiss her.

When Jenny returned in the early hours of the morning, Georgina feigned sleep, but there was very little sleep for her that night. If only she had some-one to talk to. Confide in. Someone like - Adam. She needed the comfort and strength of his arms. She'd never felt so unhappy and alone in all her life.

Chapter Five

"Georgina, wake up." Jenny shook her furiously. "Come on. We're going through the Panama today. If Pete's in a good mood we'll get to stay on the 'retreat' all day."

Georgina opened her eyes slowly and groaned. She pulled the duvet over head. "I feel terrible. I've hardly slept all night. Go away, Jenny. I want to die."

Jenny pulled the duvet back. "Well, do it tomorrow. You've *got* to see the canal. It's brill. Anyway, you can't die. You've got a little girl to think about."

Georgina sat up sharply. Oh God. She'd told Jenny about Rosie.

"Jenny, you won't... you know tell."

"Of *course* I won't. What do you think I am. Now, come on. Pete will be telling us who's got some time off. We may be lucky cos you've got the cocktail party and I'll be busy in the lounges. Our passengers will want cosseting tonight. They'll have had *such* a hard day sitting on the decks all day while we go through the Panama."

Georgina laughed and jumped out of bed, feeling suddenly that everything would be OK. She was confident that Jenny wouldn't let her down and that Hugh had nothing to gain by revealing their secret.

"What's the 'retreat', Jenny?"

"Of course, you've not been down there yet, have you? It's one of the lower decks at the stern. It's out of bounds to passengers so we can relax without being overlooked or overheard. It's just for Pete's people, hairdressers and, you know, other staff. Some officers join us occasionally. Let's go and see Pete. See if we've been lucky."

"Right folks." Pete looked around. "Everyone here? Good. Anna, Dave, Jenny, Georgina. Free till tea-time. Then bring your arses back.

You'll be serving afternoon tea for all those inside. The lads will all be busy serving passengers on the promenade deck."

"He means the stewards and waiters," whispered Jenny to Georgina.

"Come on, lets go."

"Georgina." Georgina stopped sharply in her track. "Stay."

"Oh dear. See you later, George." Jenny muttered.

Pete beckoned Georgina to him and looked at her closely. "You OK now?"

She nodded, mutely.

"Off you go then. And - don't ever ask again for time off. And Georgina, you will *not* go ashore in Acapulco. You can make up the time you lost by working on board. Understood?"
He marched off without waiting for a reply and Georgina sped swiftly to catch up with the rest of them.

Jenny was already back in their cabin, busily sorting out something to wear.

"You'll need to cover up well, George."

"Why?" Georgina sounded surprised.

"Mosquitoes. Hope you've had all your jabs, especially anti-malaria? The little bastards are only supposed to start coming out in the evening but you can't take any chances. Come on, throw something on. We've got to make the most of free time. Tell you what, I'm glad we're not working on the deck. It'll be murder, all pushing and shoving to get the best view with their cameras. The cruising fraternity are incredibly selfish."

The pair were the first to arrive at the retreat, closely followed by several others who'd been given the morning off.
Anna and Dave joined them and the four settled down to enjoy their short spell of freedom.

"Has anybody any plans for Acapulco," enquired Dave. "George, what about you?"

"I'm grounded. I'm to stay on board to make up for lost time. I won't see the cliff divers. I really wanted to see them."
Georgina looked around the group, expecting to hear words of sympathy, but none came. No-one ever questioned Pete's authority.

"I've got the port guide here, Georgina." Dave fished around in his pocket.

"You can read all about them," he added.

"Not quite the same though, is it?"

"Read it out to her, Dave. Practise being a travel agent when you leave the ship" said Jenny, opening a book. "Do it quietly though. I want to read."

"Go on, Dave," urged Georgina. "Tell me."

"Well," Dave began, enthusiastically, "they stand on the edge of the cliff and pray for about a minute and then they dive from a height of, I think about a hundred and thirty feet into a small crevice which is only eleven feet deep. And then, they climb up hundreds of stairs and do it all again."

"Gosh," gasped Georgina. "They must get well paid for it. It sounds suicidal."

"Well, they don't, you see. They charge a small admission fee and then rely on tips from tourists."

"Oh Christ, Einstein, give it a rest, will you?" Anna yawned.

"Never mind her, Dave." Georgina moved closer to him." I don't know much about the Panama Canal either. How long will it take to sail through."

"About nine hours, George." Dave was about to enjoy talking about the canal.

Anna and Jenny moaned. "Oh Lord. Don't bore her with a load of statistics, Dave. She only wanted to know how long it takes."

Dave looked hurt, and Georgina quickly jumped to his defence.

"No, go on, Dave. I'm really interested."

"Well, it's the biggest short-cut in the world, taking us from the Atlantic into the Pacific."

Jenny and Anna threw towels over their heads as Dave warmed to the subject.

"We've got to be pulled through the locks by mules and then we sail through a magnificent lake, Gatun Lake it's called. Then other locks and lakes until we reach Balbao."

"But how on *earth* can donkeys pull a ship this size."

There was an incredulous silence for a few seconds and then the three others collapsed into peals of hysterical laughter.

Georgina stared at them in amazement. "What is it. What are you all laughing at?"

Dave wiped his eyes. "Ah, come on. We're being cruel. George, when I said mules, I meant mechanical mules. They pull us along like... well... donkeys".

They starting laughing again and Georgina could feel herself blushing, a habit which was the bane of her life.

Anna stopped suddenly. "She must be joking. No-one can be that stupid. Anyway, I'm bored. Georgina, amuse us. Tell us the story of your life."

Jenny flashed Georgina a warning glance and mouthed silently.

"Careful. She's a gab-shit."

Georgina nodding her thanks, saying brightly, "Nothing to tell, really. I learned to dance and sing and got a job in the West-end. Then this job. End of story."

"Ah, come on. Got to be more than that." Anna wasn't going to give up.

Georgina thought for a minute. "OK. I went to the theatre with my mum and dad when I was about three. I kept dancing in the isles and when I got home, my mum took me to the doctors. Thought I had St Vitus dance or something. The doctor persuaded my mum to send me to dancing classes. When I was fourteen, I won a competition and the prize was an audition with a touring company. They offered me a place but one of the girls told my mum that she once had to go on stage with wet knickers cos they had no where to dry clothes. My mum marched up to the boss and said, "My daughter's not going to go on stage with wet knickers. Not for anyone." I was mortified. Anyway, I did join the company and went on from there and well - here I am."

"Tell you what. Wet knickers wouldn't have bothered Jenny. She'd just have gone on without. She's more often without than with anyway. Especially now the Scotsman's back on the scene."

Jenny smiled sweetly at Anna. "Jealous cow."

"Pack it in, you two. Stand up, George. I'll show you the mules and then let's all go swimming. The pools will be empty."

"You go, Dave. I can't be bothered." Jenny turned to Georgina. "What are you going to wear at the cocktail party tonight?"

"She'll have to wear her uniform. Adam Reynolds soon put you back where you belong didn't he, Georgina?"

"No, she won't have to wear uniform, clever dick. I didn't when I went to one. She's going to wear her own clothes."

Anna sniffed. "I doubt if she's got any suitable."

"Think I will go swimming. Come on George. There's a nasty smell around here."

Jenny took hold of Georgina's arm, dragging her away from Anna. "Don't let her bother you, George. She's jealous of you."

"Why on earth should she be jealous of me?"

"The Reynolds bloke. Says she fancies him like crazy."

"Jenny, what *do* I wear at this cocktail party?"

Jenny frowned. "I'm not sure. I've never been asked to attend one but I wasn't going to tell Anna. I suppose technically you'll be on duty so you should wear uniform, but quite frankly, if I were you, I'd wear your red velvet."

Georgina looked doubtful. "Do you really think so?"

"If you want this Reynolds fellow, George, don't miss a trick. Look your best at every opportunity. Go and have your hair done differently. Surprise him."

"Jenny, I'm not out to get him. He won't want such as me. You said

yourself, he's in another league. And his sister hates me. I daren't upset her."
Jenny leaned on her elbow and looked down at her. "You said you loved him. Well, get him into your bed. On *your* terms."
"It's not like that."
Jenny laughed shortly. "He's a fella, isn't he? 'Course it's like that. Hi, Jock. Come and meet George."
Georgina held her breath as Hugh Campbell approached them. Jenny jumped up and ran towards him. He put his arms around her and kissed her, and, catching Georgina's eyes over Jenny's shoulders, gave her a slight wink. Disconcerted, Georgina stood up to leave.
"Don't go, please. You'll be the George I've heard so much about."
Jenny pulled away from him. "Jock, meet my best friend, Georgina. I want you two to be friends."
"We will, won't we Georgina? Why, I feel as if I've known her for ages already."
Georgina glanced at him sharply, but he was smiling at her kindly and his eyes said, "Don't worry. It's our secret."
Relieved, Georgina smiled back, including Jenny in the warmth of her smile.
"I'll leave you two love birds. I've things to do."
She walked away and Jenny called after her, "Don't forget what I said, George. Go get your hair done."

Georgina placed a wrap around her shoulders, still undecided what to wear that evening. As she passed one of the small lounges on her way back to her cabin, she heard the sound of a piano being played. One of her favourite pieces, Sugar Plum Fairy from Tchaikovski's Nut Cracker Suite. Peeping round the door, she saw that the room was deserted except for the pianist, whose face was hidden by the raised lid of the grand piano. Creeping in quietly, Georgina found a large settee, curled up in the corner, and closed her eyes, delighting in the beautiful sound. The mood of the music changed and Georgina found herself listening to a piece by Mozart, followed by the lovely strains of Clare de Lune.

As the music faded, she murmured softly, "If music be the food of love, play on."

"Shakespeare. Twelfth night."
She opened her eyes to see Adam Reynolds standing over her, smiling. Forgetting her previous anger, she smiled back at him and for a moment, they were kindred spirits, delighting in the joy of music.

"Was that you playing?" He nodded. "It was lovely." She spoke softly.
"You play very well."
"You like music, Georgina?" He sat down beside her.
"Yes - yes, I do. Very much. I don't play an instrument, but I love to listen. And, of course, my dancing has given me an appreciation of all music. Mr Reynolds..."
"Adam, please." He took hold of one her hands, touching each of her fingers gently.
"You should learn to play the piano, Georgina."
"Adam," she persisted. "Why am I working at your cocktail party this evening? Why did you ask for me?" He remained silent.
"Why, Adam? Is it to - put me in my place?"
"Georgina, don't you know? I never have the chance to see you. You're either working or with the gangling youth."
Georgina took a deep breath in readiness to defend Dave.
"I'm sorry," he added swiftly. "You're very loyal. I shouldn't have said that. But he's not for you, Georgina."
Georgina recalled Old Mother Riley's words and smiled sadly.
Adam took hold of both her hands. "I want you there this evening just so that I can look at you. I want to find out why my heart pounds and my legs turn to jelly whenever you're around. I want to find out why a slip of a girl like you can fill me with such immense joy. Why I hear music when you speak. I want to find out why I love you so much. Why I should want you to become an intrinsic part of my life."
Georgina gasped. A declaration of love was the last thing she'd expected. She was almost afraid to look at him in case she should see some expression of amusement in his face. In case he was merely whiling away his time on what may be to him a boring passage. Perhaps she was expected to play the love game. Jenny would know what to do in these circumstances.
Slowly, almost tearfully she lifted her eyes to meet his. There was no mocking laughter there. His hazel eyes revealed a sincerity and tenderness that was unmistakable.
"Oh Adam, I want to love you too. But I can't. You don't know anything about me."
He took hold of her shoulders and stared deeply into her eyes.
"You can't *want* to love someone, Georgina. You either love a person or you don't."

Georgina freed herself and stood up. "I must go," she whispered. "I have to work."
She ran out of the lounge and down the gangway towards her cabin, straight into the path of a surprised officer.

"Miss, I think I've warned you..."

Taking hold of his hands, she swung him round. "Isn't it a *lovely* day, officer? I'm so happy."
She continued on her way, leaving behind a bemused and bewildered Captain, shaking his head and thinking that perhaps it was time he retired.

Georgina was on cloud nine when she reached her cabin. "I want to find out why I love you so much." That's what he'd said. She picked up Rosie's picture and stared at her beautiful daughter. Her beautiful, innocent child. She sat down heavily, her elation short lived. She must tell him before their relationship developed any further, which she knew it would. Did he love her enough to be able to accept that she had a child? That she had, if not lied to him, certainly not volunteered this important information. If he didn't, then she would lose him. In which case, would it not be all for the best?

Replacing the picture on the dressing table, Georgina closed her eyes and remembered how she had thrilled to the touch of his fingers holding hers, his loving eyes gazing into hers, searching deep into her very soul for some glimmer of reciprocation. And she knew that he'd found it. He knew that she loved him.

"I can't let him go," she told herself fiercely. "I deserve a little happiness. I love him, I want him. Oh, dear Lord, I *need* him to love me."

Ignoring an awesome feeling of betrayal, Georgina determinately put Rosie's photograph away in a drawer, covering it carefully with her underclothes.

"I'll make it up to you, sweetheart. I promise."
Her mind was made up. They had weeks yet of being together. A chance to discover one another. Perhaps then - Georgina refused to allow herself to think any further than that. From now on, she was free. Free to live and love as she pleased. To follow her heart. No-one knew about Rosie. Except Jenny. Ah, but Jenny had promised. She wouldn't tell anyone. But try as she may, Georgina couldn't forget old Mrs Riley's words. "Don't tell anyone a secret that you don't want all the ship to know."

Taking Jenny's advice, Georgina decided that she would wear her red velvet dress. She knew that Adam had liked it, and she'd made an appointment to have her hair done in the ship's hairdressing salon. She never needed, except for an occasional trim, to visit the hairdressers, thinking that in her case it was an unnecessary luxury. On this occasion, however she decided that, as she was entitled as a member of staff to a concessionary price, she was not wasting Rosie's money. Since putting away the little girl's picture, Georgina had made a resolution that all the money she earned on this cruise would be put away for her. She was only too aware that she was easing her conscience, but she was determined to develop her relationship with Adam to its ultimate conclusion, whatever that may be.

At six that evening, Georgina stood in front of the dressing table mirror and smoothed her dress over her slim hips.

"Do a twirl," commanded Jenny.

Georgina laughingly obliged. "How do I look? Is my hair alright?"

The hairdresser had asked Georgina to give her carte blanche with her hair, delighting in the gloriousness of her unspoiled blue-black tresses, and resulting in a devastatingly dramatic effect which had Jenny gasping in wonder.

"Fan-*tas*-tic. Honestly, George, you look like a film star." Georgina stared at her unfamiliar reflection in the mirror.

"I'm - not sure that I like it, Jenny. It's - not me, is it?"

"You go in there and sock it to them, gal. That cocktail party'll be full of toffee-nosed arse aches. Middle-aged mamas trying to pull their bellies in. Mutton dressed as lamb. They spend a fortune on clothes and not one of them'll be able to hold a candle to you. They'll hate you." Jenny smiled with wicked satisfaction. "Their husbands, dirty old bastards, will touch your tits, thinking that no-one will notice. But the wives always do. You'll be a sensation."

"Jenny," began Georgina, nervously. "That's not what I want. I just want to do my job properly."

She didn't add that she also wanted to see Adam, to let him know that, yes, she loved him. That she was his whenever he wanted her. That she wanted the two of them to learn about each other, to respect each other and then, perhaps for her to have sufficient confidence in their mutual love to be able to tell him about Rosie.

"Off you go. I'm having a visitor while you're out, so don't rush back."

"Who?" questioned Georgina.

"King-Kong," retorted Jenny, sarcastically. "Who do *you* think?"

As the cabin door closed heavily behind her, Georgina breathed a sigh of relief. Her decision to hide away Rosie's photograph had been vindicated. If

Hugh had seen it, he'd have put two and two together. He would have known that Rosie was his. That she hadn't miscarried. She hoped and prayed that Jenny would not betray her. She was beginning to realize more than ever that Jenny and Hugh together spelt disaster for her. She was now relying on *both* of them keeping a secret. And - she felt that, as a friend, she should be warning Jenny about Hugh - her Jock's - drinking. But how could she, without revealing that he was her ex-lover?

Eve Reynolds' state room was gradually filling with specially selected guests. Jenny had explained to Georgina that cocktail parties on board a cruise ship were a ritual peculiar to the seasoned voyager and that they normally involved the older persons. Each person present would, in turn, hold a party in their cabin. These gatherings were considered to be extremely prestigious, depending on the importance of the host and there was great competition amongst the lesser mortals to wangle an invitation to one where the Captain was to be present. To achieve this was the pinnacle. The highlight of the cruise. All this jockeying to be in the presence of the 'great one', was viewed with amused tolerance by the younger set of passengers on whom the shipping company's now rely heavily to fill their ships, Even more amusing was the fact that everyone aboard the ship, regardless of status, wealth or connection, was invited to 'Captains Cocktail Party.' Free drinks and nuts for everyone and a hand shake from the man himself.

"There's also," Jenny had continued, "the invitation card. "The Captain requests the pleasure of..." Jenny laughed. "Can you imagine those poor unfortunates back home having it pushed under their noses and being regaled with stories of 'when I was at the captain's party,' as if they were the selected few."

Georgina smilingly recalled Jenny's cynical comments as she looked around the assembled crowd. The women were middle-aged, mostly overweight and definitely overdressed and bejewelled and in the majority. Twice as many females to males, which seemed to bear out another of Jenny's wicked comments that as soon as the husband died, the widow hopped on to a ship and proceeded to spend the insurance money.

Georgina, handing round the silvered trays of canapés was in great demand by the males who seemed to have developed an insatiable appetite for the delightful morsels of toast, covered with creamed cheese, prawns, caviar and anchovy. It was with undisguised relief that she saw Adam enter the state room. He caught her eye and, rolling his eyes in obvious amusement at the scene, strolled over to her, authoritatively dispersing the white tuxedoed males, who were already showing signs of having partaken too freely of a never ending supply of alcohol. Silently, he guided her to a corner of the room, taking the tray from her and handing it to a bewhiskered elderly gentleman.

"You don't mind do you, sir. Can't get the staff these days, you know." Georgina giggled and Adam placed his hand over her mouth.

"Let's get out of here. I want to kiss you, my darling." Georgina's body trembled with desire.

"Adam, I love you. I want you so much."

"How dare you come to work dressed like that?"

Eve Reynolds tapped Georgina on the shoulder. "Go to your cabin and change into your uniform. You're *not* an invited guest You're supposed to be working here this evening."

Georgina knew that she was being deliberately insulting and turned to Adam, confidently expecting him to tell his sister not to speak to her in that manner, but to her consternation, he walked away, leaving her to the wrath of Eve. As Georgina walked towards the door, biting her lips in a determined effort not to lose her temper and retaliate, Adam called out to her. With great relief, she turned to him, expectantly.

"Miss Murphy, pour me a gin and tonic before you go!"

Georgina walked wearily to her cabin. He'd done it again. Made it clear to her that it was all a game, and that she was the pawn. She didn't understand this way of life, and she now decided that she didn't want to. Love, or the pretence of love was cheap in the insular life on board a ship and Georgina wanted no part of it. She'd been ready to give herself freely to Adam Reynolds and he'd thrown her commitment to him back in her face. Georgina was filled with embarrassment and humiliation as she recalled how she had made it clear to him that she would have gone to bed with him there and then. That she hungered for his touch. He was probably at this moment having a good laugh with his friends, telling them of his conquest of her, boasting that he could pull the girls. And those old men, with their hot, groping fingers would be licking their lips, listening with envy to the exploits of a younger man.

The waste bucket was outside the cabin door. Jenny had her Jock in with her. What was she to do? She needed to gain access to change into her uniform. She leaned on the wall, confused and uncertain what to do. She couldn't bang on the door. Jenny was entitled to her privacy, having warned her that the cabin would be 'occupied'.

Turning sharply on her heels, Georgina resolutely walked towards the bar. She wouldn't go back. Why should she? She didn't care if she was reported. If the company was so petty as to dismiss her on the whim of Eve Reynolds, then so be it. She could always go back to the West End. The choreographer had told her that there would always be a place for her. Anyway, she didn't want to see Adam Reynolds. She didn't want to see him ever again, and if he thought that she was going to keep him amused in Los Angeles, he was sadly mistaken. Her rage rose again. He could ask that fat cow, the nympho to go with him. Jenny was right. He wasn't her sort.

"Hi, Georgina. Gosh, you look gorgeous. I thought you were serving the toffs this evening?"

"Hello, Dave. Yes I was... I... er ... left early. Dave, what are you doing when we get to Los Angeles?"

He shrugged his shoulders. "Nothing. Why?"

"Can I go ashore with you, please. I understand that we shouldn't wander off alone."

"That would be great," he said eagerly. "No, you're right. It can be a bit dicey for a woman on her own. It's quite a long way from the harbour, but the company usually provide some transport into the city. The City of Angels. Hey, we'll go to the Hollywood bowl. We'll dance on the stage, you and I. I'll take your picture and you can show it to all your friends." Dave laughed. "You don't have to tell them that there was no audience."

"What's the Hollywood bowl?"

"It's the famous open air amphitheatre. It's always open. We can just go on to the stage. It'll be fun, Georgina. And I'll take you to Mann's Chinese Theatre. You must have heard of that. It's where all the hand prints, foot prints, even nose prints of celebrities are placed in the concrete. Maybe our footprints will be there someday."

Georgina smiled at Dave's enthusiasm. How refreshingly different, she thought, to the lordly sarcasm of Adam Reynolds and his contemporaries.

"That'll be lovely, Dave. I'll really look forward to it. You - don't mind my asking you, do you, Dave? You're sure you weren't going with anyone?" Dave gazed at her, a serious expression now on his face. "Georgina, I'm - in love with you. You must know that. You're the most beautiful girl I've ever seen. I know that you've no feelings for me, but... well - we've a long way to go yet. Perhaps... well - perhaps before the end of the cruise you may find that you like me a little."

Georgina sighed. "Dave, I have - responsibilities. I - can't love anyone, but I do like you. I like you a lot. Can we just leave it at that for now? Please." Out of the corner of her eye, Georgina saw Adam Reynolds approaching the now crowded bar.

"Dave, I'd like to buy you a drink." Calling the barman over, Georgina placed her order. "Lots of ice, please."

"Georgina, come and sit down. I want to speak to you."

Adam took hold of her arm, but Georgina freed herself and taking the gin and tonic from the barman, stood on the tip of her toes and poured it over Adam Reynold's head.

"Your gin and tonic *Sir,*" she said sweetly. "Dave darling, I'll see you later."

Georgina saw with relief that the waste bucket had been taken in. Hugh had left. Opening the cabin door, she called to Jenny, "Are you in?"

"I'm in the shower. Shan't be a mo'."

Georgina stood in front of the mirror and began brushing her hair, furiously.

"Hey, what's wrong with you?"

Jenny stepped out of the shower room, wrapped in a large white fluffy towel.

"You know, George, one thing I always miss when I'm not on a ship are the towels. God knows how they get them so soft. Now, what's eating you? You've ruined that hairstyle."

"Jenny, I've had it up to here." Georgina made a cutting movement across her neck.

"So have I, darling," laughed Jenny. "It was great." Catching sight of her friends face, Jenny stopped laughing.

"What is it? What's happened?"

Georgina lowered the hairbrush, sat down on her bunk and told her what she'd done.

Jenny whistled and shook her head. "They'll send you home. What made you do it, you idiot?"

"I wanted to."

"Christ, Georgina," Jenny exploded, impatiently. "We all want to do things like that from time to time. But we don't. Not if we want to keep our jobs. Why let a man like Reynolds get under your skin. I *told* you. *Use* the bastards. Look, you'd better get changed. The show starts in less than half-an-hour. You'd better not be late. I'll wait for you. I want to make sure you don't get into anymore trouble."

The two girls hurriedly changed into the costumes for their first number and lined up on the stage with the rest of the dancers, most of whom flashed Georgina a sympathetic glance. Anna leaned forward as they arrived.

"I hear you couldn't hold your drink, Georgina."

Georgina remained silent, and even Jenny could not think of a suitable reply. Pete, the MC for the evening was already out front going through his routine before announcing the dancers. He finished to the usual round of applause and as the curtain was pulled back, he caught sight of Georgina.

"You," he whispered pointing a finger at her ominously. "In the boardroom straight after the show."

"Oh Lord," groaned Jenny. "This is it, girl."

It was almost eleven-o-clock before the show finished, by which time Georgina was beyond caring what happened to her. She'd resigned herself to the fact that she was finished. That Eve Reynolds must have been correct in her analysis of her. She was not the right kind of material to work on a cruise ship.

Normally after the show, whilst the dancers were free to do as they pleased, Pete's people, the Cruise Director's team, remained on duty, mingling with passengers and being generally helpful and pleasant. Dave, Anna and Jenny, now changed into evening dress gathered around her, back stage. Georgina, considering herself to be dismissed had changed into jeans and T-shirt.

"You were quite magnificent," said Dave, in an effort to cheer her up.

"Don't be bloody stupid, Dave," interjected Jenny, sharply. "Don't encourage her. She behaved like a spoilt child. Now, listen to me. Your only chance is to tell Pete that you had a mental blackout or something. That you can't remember doing it. Don't - for God's sake tell him what you told me. That you did it because you wanted to."

"What had he done to you?" asked Anna, curiously.

"Shut up, Anna. Georgina, go and see Pete now and *grovel.*"

Georgina stood up, defiantly. "I won't beg. I don't want to stay. I shall get a flight home from Los Angeles. We'll be there in two day's, won't we? I'll probably join a nunnery," she finished, mournfully.

Her three colleagues burst out laughing at her expression.

"You can't," replied Jenny, dropping her eyes.

"Why not?" asked Anna.

Georgina flashed Jenny a warning glance, fearful that she was going to mention Rosie.

But Jenny smiled and shook her head. "You'd never get all that hair inside a wimple."

Dave took hold of her hand. "Come on. I'll walk to the board room with you."

They walked in silence and as they approached the door, Dave kissed her cheek and left her.

"Come." Pete's voice called out loudly as she knocked on the door.

He leaned back in his chair, balancing it on its two back legs and viewed her through narrowed eyes.

As she opened her mouth to speak, Pete bellowed at her, "Not a *word.* What - did you think you were about? You should be able to deal with randy fellows at your age without resorting to anointing them with bleeding gin and tonics. You've been in show business long enough to know what to expect. You're a lovely girl. You're going to have men chasing you. If you want to teach them a lesson, kick 'em in the balls if you like - but when no one's *looking.* To react as you did in a public bar is indefensible. You realise that what you did is a dismissible offence?"

Georgina gasped. "What are you saying, Pete? It's nothing to do with... randy fellows."

Pete continued, ignoring her outburst. "Fortunately, Adam Reynolds has admitted that he has been - bothering you - sexually. He feels that your action, albeit unorthodox, was fully justified. He says he thinks he pushed you beyond reasonable limits and sends his apologies. He has asked me to keep you on. Off you go back to work."

Georgina left the board room bemused. Why had Adam Reynolds lied for her? He had never harassed her. She must speak to him. She wandered from bar to bar, the casino, library, lounges, but he was nowhere to be found.

"George, there you are. What happened?" Jenny grabbed hold of her.

"I'm to stay."

"Oh, that's great. Come on. I'll buy you a drink. Gin and tonic OK?"

The girls laughed and joined Anna and Dave in the late night bar.

"Friends in high places?" inquired Anna, mockingly.

"No, Anna. Pete just couldn't afford to lose real talent." Georgina was learning to hold her own in the cruising world.

"Think I'll give Jock a rest tonight." Jenny yawned as the two girls undressed. "Keep you company. Anyway, I'm knackered myself. Goodnight George. I'm ever so pleased you're staying. You can tell me tomorrow how

you swung it."
Georgina lay awake, listening to her friends steady breathing. Although the cabin was air conditioned, she was hot, restless, unable to sleep. The thought of Adam defending her once again disturbed her. She didn't want any favours from anyone. The air in the cabin was stifling and, slipping a robe over her naked body, she carefully opened the cabin door. Perhaps a few minutes out on the deck would cool her down and help her to sleep.

The Starlight glided swiftly and silently through the dark waters of the Pacific Ocean, most of its human cargo fast asleep, placing its trust in the massive hunk of metal carrying them to the next port of call, confident of the skills of the ship's personnel.

Georgina leaned on the rails, a cool breeze teasing the small tendrils of hair on her forehead. An officer walked by, turning his head to look at her.

"You OK Miss?"

"Yes. Yes - I'm fine. Just cooling down a little. I'm going back in now."

Smiling at her, with nocturnal sympathy, he said, "I would if I were you. It can feel a bit spooky out here on your own. And there could be pirates around."

Georgina shivered at the thought as she walked along the gangway. Glancing over her shoulder, she felt fear rising within her. Adam's cabin was a few paces away. Quickening her pace, she recalled how, at the cocktail party, he'd put his hand over her mouth. How she'd thrilled to his touch. She remembered the tingling in her spine when he had said he wanted to kiss her. And she knew that she wanted him. She wanted him now. She didn't care if he was only using her. Her desire for him became overwhelming. Reaching the cabin, she knocked gently on the door. There was no reply. She knocked again, a little louder, and the door swung open.

He stood in the doorway, fastening the belt on his white towelling bath robe.

"Adam, please - don't laugh at me. I'm - a bit frightened and - I love you so much."

He took hold of her arm and pulled her inside, holding her close to him. "Georgina, why should I laugh at you? Surely you know how much I love you."

Slowly, he unfastened her robe, letting it fall to the floor. As she stood naked in front of him, he caught his breath and touched her breasts gently.

"Georgina, darling. You're the loveliest woman I've ever seen."

She gazed lovingly at his tousled dark brown hair, his hazel eyes, heavy

with sleep. The muscles in his broad shoulders rippled as he removed his white robe, revealing a slim waist and narrow hips.
Georgina averted her eyes in some confusion as he stood naked in front of her.
"Don't turn away from me, Georgina. There's nothing to hide between us. No secrets."
Georgina shivered as he said that. No secrets. Yet she knew that she dare not tell him. Not yet.
"No secrets Adam."
She put her arms around his waist, pressing her body close to his, sensing the passion rising between them.
"Are you sure about this, Georgina?" he whispered, his lips close to her ear. Are you sure this is what you want?"
"I've never been so sure about anything in my life."
He lilted her up in his arms and, placing her down gently on his bed, he lay down beside her, drawing her to him with a desire matched only by her own. They made love and promised undying, eternal love until the pale fingers of dawn stretched through the porthole and across their bodies and then they slept, wrapped in each others arms.
Georgina awoke to find Adam leaning on his elbow, looking down at her.
"I've been willing you to wake up for nearly an hour." He smiled down at her.
"Why?" she asked, sleepily.
"To tell you I love you."
Georgina turned her slim body towards him. "You could have woken me up. Why didn't you? We have wasted a whole hour. Love me now, Adam," she whispered.
He touched her hair and lifting a ruffled curl, tickled her nose.
"You're a wanton, brazen hussy," he teased. "You must arise, maiden."
Georgina sat up and bent her knees, clasping her hands around them.
"Adam, tell me. Why did you let your sister speak to me in that manner at the cocktail party? Why were you so awful to me, after saying that you wanted to kiss me? And you told Pete that you had pestered me. Why"?
"How could I let you fly away out of my life? I had to keep you here, Georgina until I was sure of your feelings. And at the cocktail party, I wasn't sure how our relationship was going to develop. If I'd defended you in front of all those people, they would have realised that I was - interested in you." He smiled and kissed her lightly on her shoulder. "You have your work here

to consider and, being the kind of people they are, they could have made life very difficult for you. Now - it doesn't matter anymore. Marry me, my love and the rest of the world can go to hell."

There was a knock on the cabin door. Georgina gasped. "Who will that be?"

"Only the steward with tea. Don't worry."

Adam swung his legs out of bed, slung his robe around his shoulders and opened the door. Eve Reynolds pushed her way in.

"I knew you had someone in here, Adam." She glared at Georgina. "You little tramp. Get out. At once. I knew you were a trollop the minute I set eyes on you."

Georgina's lips quivered. "Adam, please," she whispered tremulously.

"Don't let her..."

"Eve, you go too far. Georgina and I are going to be married." Eve Reynolds stared at him, her face expressionless, then, turning on her heel left without saying another word.

"Adam, what if she tells..."

Adam became impatient. "Forget her. She's - of no consequence."

"How can you *say* that? She's your sister. And - a director."

"Georgina, do you want to shower here?" Georgina sensed that Adam was suddenly distant. He wanted rid of her.

"No, I'll go back to my cabin."

"Off you go then. Here, put your robe on. Run now."

Georgina fastened the robe tightly round her. "Captain says I mustn't run," she said primly.

Adam relaxed and remarked laughingly, "It's not like you, Irish, to bow to authority."

"Where've you *been*?" Jenny was sitting up in bed, drinking a cup of tea.

"I've been worried sick.``

"I - can't say."

"Course you can. I'm your mate."

Georgina remained silent.

"Have you been away all night?" Jenny persisted. "You might as well tell me. I won't let up till you do."

Georgina sighed. "I - spent the night with Adam. Adam Reynolds." Jenny almost choked on her tea.

"Georgina Murphy, if you were Japanese and male, you'd be a Kamikaze pilot."

Chapter Six

The Starlight had left the Panama canal behind and was sailing confidently and majestically, haughtily in command of the gentle, passive swell of the North Pacific Ocean, the battering by the vicious Atlantic waves at the other side of the canal forgotten .

Acapulco had been visited, the golden beaches admired and reluctantly left behind, the traditionalists raved about the joys of downtown old Acapulco and now everyone was looking forward to Los Angeles. They were due to dock in a couple of hours and most passengers were having an early breakfast so that they could spend as much time as they could in the city.

Once, cruising meant spending two, even three days in one port, but the modern trend is to visit as many ports as possible and today, most of the trips ashore are whistle-stop, arriving early in the morning and leaving minutes before midnight on that same day. There were several organised tours from the ship. A trip to Disneyland, the Getty Museum, Sunset Boulevard, a visit to Universal Studios, so many famous places that Georgina had only been able to dream about, never envisaging a time when she would actually see them.

She'd seen nothing of Adam since spending the night together, and during the following day's routine sometimes wondered if she'd dreamt it all. But then she remembered his burning kisses, his searching tongue, strong arms that had held her passionately, demanding, yet gentle. And she'd responded to his passion in a way that she had never thought possible. A passion that had left her reeling and light headed, uncaring of the consequences of their union. Momentarily, a vague thought had passed through her mind. A thought echoed and spoken by Jenny.

"George." Jenny had watched her speculatively as she'd dressed after spending the night with Adam.

"You are on the pill, aren't you?"

"Of course," she'd replied, indignantly. "You must think I'm stupid."

But Georgina was not 'on the pill'. Georgina hadn't come on this cruise with any intentions of having any sexual relationships.

"You're sure? Cos the Doc'll give you something if you do it quickly."

"No, It's alright, Jenny. I'm OK Honest. Anyway, he wants to..." She stopped.

"Marry you," Jenny interrupted scornfully. "That's what they all say, darling. Does he know about Rosie?"

"No, no-one knows except you."

"Then how can you say you'll marry him. He'll do his nut when he knows there's a kid. Grow up, Georgina. What are you doing in LA?"

"I don't know what to do. I think Adam's expecting me to spend the day with him, but I promised Dave I'd go with him."

"Well, you'll have to sort that out for yourself. Jock and I are going to Long beach. Jock wants to see the Queen Mary and Spruce Goose."

"What's Spruce Goose?"

"It's the world's largest aircraft. Brainchild of Howard Hughes. Not my cup of tea really, but it'll keep Jock sweet. He's been a bit iffy lately."

Georgina was immediately attentive. "What do you mean, iffy?"

"Oh, I don't know. His attention keeps wandering. He was asking about you yesterday. Hope you've not had your eye on him." Jenny fixed her with a steely gaze. "You haven't, have you?"

Georgina laughed, uncomfortably. "I've hardly seen him. Don't know him, do I?"

Jenny relaxed. "That's OK then. But remember, friendship only stretches so far when there's a bloke involved. Have a good day, George. I probably won't see you till tomorrow. Are you shacking up with Reynolds tonight?"

Georgina blushed. She still wasn't used to Jenny's free and easy approach to sex.

"I - haven't seen him since ..."

Jenny shrugged. "You're probably just a one night stand. I did warn you." She picked up her bag and left, leaving Georgina confused and frightened. What if Jenny was right? Why hadn't Adam contacted her?

Georgina slowly gathered together items she thought she would need for a full day in the heat of Los Angeles. Sun hat, sunglasses, a light weight jacket to protect her arms against the burning sun she had been warned about. She'd arranged to meet Dave outside the main lounge, which meant her walking past Adam's cabin, and as she approached the door she paused, wondering if she should knock to let him know that she was going ashore. Deciding against it, she hurried past, anxious not to keep Dave waiting, but as she did so, she was grabbed from behind. Startled, she cried out.

"Sh, it's only me." Adam pulled her into the cabin and put his arms around her. burying his head in her hair, kissing the nape of her neck. Georgina felt the blood racing in her veins, leaving her weak and helpless.

Resisting the temptation to turn around to him and press her body close to his, Georgina spoke. "Adam, I'm in a hurry. I must go."
He slipped his hand inside her blouse, his sensitive fingers gently encircling her breast. "Georgina, darling. Come to bed. To hell with LA."
"I can't. I promised Dave."
She felt his whole body stiffen and he released her.
"You were supposed to spend the day with me." His voice was harsh and accusing.
Georgina turned to face him. "I know, but... after the cocktail party and - you know - in the bar - I thought... I promised Dave I'd go with him," she finished weakly.
Adam frowned, his hazel eyes narrowing, his jaw taut. A tiny muscle in the side of his face twitched slightly.
"I don't intend sharing you, Georgina." His tone was cold and uncompromising. "Go and tell him you won't be going with him."
She stared at him in disbelief and spoke in a voice as icy as his. "I can't - *won't* do that, Adam. I'm not in the habit of breaking promises as easily as that."
Two pairs of eyes locked, two equally strong wills battled silently, neither prepared to give way. After a few seconds of determined silence, the hazel eyes softened, the stern face relaxed and the tightened lips smiled.
"I'm not used to women like you, Irish. The women I usually associate with don't know the meaning of the word, principles. Of course you must go with the *lad*." He deliberately emphasised the word, "It wouldn't be fair to disappoint him. You'd never let anyone down, would you Georgina? And I love you for it."
Georgina hesitated for a second. "Adam, when you asked me to marry you - did you mean it?"
He looked surprised. "What a question. Do you think I go around asking anyone to share my life? Of course I meant it, my darling."
"Your sister. She doesn't like me."
"You'll be marrying me, not Eve." he retorted dryly.
"Adam," she began slowly. "Adam, when I come back on board..."
"You'll come straight to me, my love," he whispered, touching her cheek with the back of his hand.
"Adam, please - listen to me. Tonight, there's something I must tell you."
"And there is so much I want to tell you, Georgina. How my life is

suddenly worth living again. How I long for your touch. How I see your lovely face wherever I go. I knew I loved you the first time I saw you, sitting in that garage, looking so unhappy. I wanted to pick you up and carry you away, Georgina. To look after you. Care for you always. For you never to cry again."

"Adam, stop - please. I need to talk to you. But later. I must go now."

Turning away from him, Georgina sped along the gangway, her heart pounding.

"I must tell him," she told herself, desperately. "I can't go on deceiving him. Oh God, please let him love me enough to accept Rosie."

"There you are. I thought you'd changed your mind." Dave smiled at her.

"Have you been rushing? You look as if you've just done a four minute mile."

"Come on, Dave. Let's get off this ship."

Georgina grabbed his arm and they both ran down the gangway, jumping on to a coach about to leave for the city.

Georgina was to discover that Dave was an absolute bundle of energy whilst on shore and by mid afternoon she was wearying. They had seen the Hollywood Hills, danced on the stage of the Hollywood bowl, inspected the Chinese Theatre and marvelled at the hand prints and foot prints of the stars.

"Dave, can we please slow down a little. Let's find a cafe and take a break. I'll treat you to tea and cakes before we attempt Sunset Boulevard and Rodeo Drive.

Dave laughed. "Sorry, Georgina. I do get carried away, I'm afraid. I've seen it all before, but it never ceases to amaze me. Listen, are you OK? You seem a bit... well... far away."

"Yes - I'm fine, Dave. It's just that - I've an important decision to make tonight."

"Anything you want to talk about?"

"No, thanks Dave. This is something I've to decide myself. Here's a place. Let's go in, shall we?"

A smiling waiter showed them to a table and Georgina thankfully sat down, easing her aching feet out of her shoes. As she did so, the table slipped away from them and there was the sound of breaking glass.

Georgina looked, around in bewilderment as the waiter shouted to them to leave. Dave grabbed hold of her hand, pulling her to her feet and they both stumbled to the door.

"What is it?" gasped Georgina. "What's happening?"

"Earthquake," responded Dave, grimly. "Let's get away from the buildings."
There was panic all around, people shouting, screaming, running, some sitting on the ground with blood on their faces as shattered windows fell about them, others wandering around as if in a trance.
"Oh, Dave. I'm frightened. My little girl. My Rosie. I'll never see her again."
She began to cry, shaking uncontrollably, and Dave slapped her sharply across her face.
"Stop that," he said sharply. "Come on, keep on moving. We must find an open space. There'll be an after quake anytime now."
They moved with the crowds and eventually found themselves sitting on a grass verge. Dave breathed a sigh of relief.
"That's it, I think. You alright, Georgina? Sorry I hit you, but I had to."
"What happened? Was it really an earthquake? I can't believe it. Are we safe now?"
"Yes, I think so. It's all over now. Relax. Lie back on the grass for a while, then we'll move on." He gazed at her anxiously. "Unless you'd rather go back to the ship."
"No - I'm fine. We'll carry on if you're sure it won't happen again."
Georgina would dearly have loved to go back. She wanted to see Adam. Make sure he was safe, but she couldn't spoil the rest of Dave's day. She knew that he wouldn't allow her to go back to the ship alone. Rising from the grass, she put her hand out to him.
"Up you get. Where do we go from here?"
"Sit down, Georgina." His voice was serious and Georgina sat down beside him quickly.
"What is it Dave? Is something wrong"?
"You said 'my little girl'. My Rosie. *Is* she your Rosie? Is she your child, Georgina?"
Georgina was silent. She hadn't realised that in her panic she'd revealed her secret.
"You don't have to tell me."
Dave's voice was gentle, kind, and Georgina began to cry again. He took her in his arms and held her close.
"Poor baby. Poor little Georgina. You still seem like a child yourself. How old were you?"
"I - was only fifteen when I fell pregnant. Sixteen when she was born. So,

not that young really." She swallowed hard, trying to stem her tears.

"And you kept her." The statement was made in a voice full of admiration.

She nodded. "Of course."

Dave remained silent, still holding her close.

"Dave." She looked up at him and with a catch in her voice said, "Could you ever take on another man's child?"

He held her away from him and asked, teasingly, "Is this a proposal, Georgina? If so - I accept."

Georgina caught her breath in alarm.

"Don't look so worried. I'm only joking. I know where your heart lies. It's Reynolds, isn't it?" She lowered her eyes and nodded. "Does he know about Rosie?"

She shook her head slowly.

"You know you'll have to tell him, Georgina."

"I'll tell him tonight. I have to. He's asked me to marry him. I should have told him before, but I was afraid."

"Georgina, if he loves you, *really* loves you, he'll accept your Rosie. It not," he shrugged his shoulders, "then you'll have had a lucky escape."

She leaned forward and kissed him. "Thanks Dave. I wish..."

"Hey, watch it, gal. I'm really a most *randy* bloke. Not to be trusted."

He playfully tickled her and they both rolled around the grass verge till Georgina was helpless with laughter.

"That's better," he said with satisfaction. "No more tears. You're too pretty to be unhappy."

She was instantly sober. "Dave - what am I going to do? Something dreadful's happened."

Alarmed, Dave took hold of her arms. "What is it, Georgina? What's happened?"

Georgina stared at him in consternation, then looked down. He followed her gaze.

"I left my shoes in the cafe."

It was late evening when Georgina and Dave returned to The Starlight. They spotted Adam Reynolds leaning on the ship's rail, obviously agitated, as he watched passengers climbing the gangway.

"I think your love awaits you, Georgina," smiled Dave. "I'll go on ahead and leave you two together."

As she stepped on to the deck, Adam stretched out his arms and she ran into them.

"Are you alright, Georgina? I've been worried sick. I didn't go ashore so I didn't know what was happening."

"Didn't you feel the earthquake on the ship?"

"No, it only causes a slight swell in the water. Georgina, we're having dinner in my cabin tonight. I want you to myself. Go and shower and change into something beautiful."

As she turned to leave, he called her back. "Irish,"

"Yes, Adam."

Bending down low, he whispered in her ear, "Don't forget to bring an overnight bag."

He grinned at her wickedly and Georgina, feeling herself starting to blush, made her escape.

Georgina sat on her bunk, her mind in a turmoil. She knew that she must tell Adam about Rosie tonight. She had to look her best. Opening the wardrobe door, she pulled out one dress after another. If only Jenny were here to help her choose. Thinking of Jenny, she was reminded of Hugh. What a coincidence, him being on this ship, And yet she knew she should not be surprised. As with all professions, theirs was a small world, and it was inevitable that she would meet up with him again sooner or later. He'd leave the ship in a couple of weeks and she could relax.

Holding a vivid orange dress in front of her, she viewed it critically in the mirror. With her luxuriant blue-black hair and green eyes, she knew that she was able to wear startling colours to good effect. Shaking her head, she replaced it. Tonight, she needed to be more subdued. Her mother had made for her a lovely cream pure silk skirt and matching top with tiny pearl buttons down the front. She'd never worn it, not even tried it on. Her mother knew her measurements well enough. This is what she would wear tonight. Adam would love its serene classic design.

With a final, satisfied glance in the mirror, Georgina opened the cabin door, then firmly closed it again. Opening the drawer of the dressing table, she took out Rosie's photograph and, with a flourishing, defiant gesture, placed it on the dressing table.

Adam's approving glance as she entered his cabin assured her that she had made the right choice. He handed her an aperitif, and as she sipped it, savouring the unfamiliar taste, she gazed around the cabin. She'd paid scant attention to it the last time she had been there. It was officially classed a stateroom and was, as one would expect, extravagantly spacious compared to hers and Jenny's. It was an outside cabin with a large picture window, through which Georgina could see the lights of Long Beach, whose night-life was about to commence. The deep piled midnight blue carpeting matched the curtains and the cushions, which were scattered on the bed. A table had been set for two people. Fanned napkins, exactly the same blue as the carpet contrasted sharply with the crisp, snow-white tablecloth, and the shining cutlery and sparkling glasses, the tiny blue flowers in a crystal vase in the centre of the table displayed an air of taste and quality that only comes with careful attention to co-ordination and detail. On a smaller table sat an ice bucket, cradling a bottle of Moet Chandon.

"This is lovely," she said, holding her glass toward him. "I don't know much about drinks. What is it?"

"It's a kir. White wine and a touch of blackcurrant. I chose the menu for you. Is that alright?"

"Yes. Yes, I don't mind. I can eat almost anything."

He placed his hands around her tiny waist. "You mean to say you don't have to diet."

"No. I suppose I use all my energy dancing. Perhaps when I stop, I might have to be a little more careful, although my mother is not much plumper than I am."

"Is your father alive, Georgina? There are so many things I want to know about you. Where do you live? What's your Irish connection? Do you have any brothers and sisters? Do you like children? Do you *want* children? I want to know everything about you, my darling. But not tonight. Tonight I shall love you. We'll dine and drink champagne and make glorious love all night."

"And you, Adam. I know nothing of you, except that I love you with all my heart. Adam - I have something..." There was a knock on the door.

"Ah, that'll be our first course."

Adam opened the door and a steward wheeled in a trolley on which was a silver salver and cover and a bottle of wine.

"We'll ring when we're ready for the next course."

Adam dismissed the steward in a manner that was neither offensive or deferent and Georgina became even more aware that this was his life style. That he had a very different background to her own.

"More wine, Adam? I mustn't drink too much. I have to work tomorrow."

"You can resign. When we're married, you won't ever have to work again."

"I can't resign. I must complete my contract."

He sighed. "Those principles again. Don't worry. I am not going to ply you with drink so that I may have my wicked way with you." He put his arms around her. "I don't need to, do I, Georgina. You do want me, don't you? As much as I want you?"
Georgina realised with surprise that this apparently confident man was doubtful of her love. and was looking for assurance. She recalled him saying his life was worth living again. He must have been hurt at sometime in his life. Badly let down. And she was going to hurt him again. As she gazed into his anxious eyes, she knew that she couldn't. Not tonight. Gently taking hold of his hands, she pulled him towards the bed.

"Let me prove to you how much I want you, Adam," she whispered.

"I think my Farfalette Marinara will be cold, Georgina," smiled Adam.

"Some wayward female kept me from it."
Georgina lifted the cover from the salver. "What a waste. It looks delicious." She stared in dismay at the pasta, prawns, crab-meat, scallops, mixed in a creamy sauce. Her frugal background had never allowed her to waste anything.

"Shall I ask the steward to warm it up?"

Adam exploded with laughter.

"I think we'll skip the first course and go straight on to the next. Anyway, my darling, I'd much rather have had the dish of our own making."
Georgina started to blush and Adam bent down and kissed the tip of her nose.

"You're really quite shy, aren't you? Don't be, Georgina. Not with me." He poured two glasses of the chilled white wine. "I'll order the main course, shall I?"

"Yes please," replied Georgina. "I'm suddenly very hungry. What are we having?"

"If making love makes you hungry, child, you are going to finish up a very fat lady, indeed. We are having Fillet of Salmon, grilled in butter, followed by Tiramisu."

"What's Tiramisu?" she asked curiously.

"Sponge, with cream cheese soaked in coffee liqueur."

"You seem to be very knowledgeable about food, Adam. Can you cook?"

"I spent two years at a catering college to satisfy my father that I was capable of doing something other than playing the piano. I'm afraid my father didn't consider making music was work."

He remained pensively silent for a while. Georgina watched him thoughtfully. He was not aware that she knew something of his childhood. That Mrs Riley had told her of the tragic death of his parents and of his sister Eve's unfortunate encounter with a ship's engineer.

She decided that he would tell her of these happenings if he wanted to. In the meantime, her feelings for him were becoming more and more intense. She would tell him tomorrow about Rosie. She must find out if his feelings for her were strong enough to endure the shock of knowing that she had a child.

Georgina awoke the following morning not quite knowing where she was. Stretching her arm across the bed, she smiled as she felt the warmth where Adam's body had lain. She felt an unexpected rush of passion surge through her as she recalled the night of love they had shared and as Adam emerged from the shower room, she held her arms out to him. He sat on the bed and took her in his arms.

"It's late, Georgina. If you really want to go to work, it's time you left my bed. And if you don't stop looking at me like that, my lovely, you are going to be very late for work."

She gasped. "What's the time?"

He threw back the bed cover, revealing her naked, beautifully formed body. Kneeling at the side of the bed, he leaned over her and kissed her naval.

"Who cares?" he murmured.

Ignoring all the rules, Georgina ran along the gangway, down the stairs and quickly unlocked her cabin.

"Are you in, Jenny? I'm awfully late."

"Jenny's in the laundry room."

Hugh was standing in front of the dressing table, holding Rosie's picture. Georgina gasped, horror stricken.

"What are you doing here? Give that to me." She held out her hand for the photograph, but he held it away from her.

"She's mine, isn't she? You didn't lose the baby. You lied, Georgina. Why? This is my child. You've kept her from me."

"It would have been pointless, Hugh. I didn't want to marry you. I didn't want to marry anyone. I - I was too young. It - was - easier not to tell you. No complications. I've looked after her," she added, defensively. "She's wanted for nothing."

"Except a father, Georgina. What do you tell her when she asks where her daddy is?"

Angrily, she turned on him. "You didn't want a baby, Hugh. You could have found us if you had really wanted to. You haven't told Jenny, have you?" she asked, fearfully.

"Told Jenny what?"

Georgina spun round. Jenny was standing in the doorway, clutching her laundry bag close to her chest.

"What are you two up to?" she asked, suspiciously. "What have you got there, Jock?"

Slowly, he replaced the silver framed photograph back on the dressing table. Jenny picked it up and stared at the child's smiling face. Lifting her head, she looked through narrowing eyes first at Georgina and then at Hugh. With a reluctantly dawning realisation, she threw the picture on to Georgina's bunk, and with a howl reminiscent of a banshee, threw herself at Hugh, pummelling his chest with clenched fists.

"You bastard. You dirty Scottish bastard."

He grabbed her wrists and pushed her away from him.

Georgina took hold of her arm. "Jenny - please - stop, Jenny."

Jenny drew back and dealt her a stinging blow across the face. Georgina, caught of balance, fell to the floor.

"You *cow,*" spat Jenny, leaning over her. "You simpering, hypocritical little cow. You've pretended to be so innocent. So naive. And all the time you and - Hugh - I suppose you've been shagging behind my back, haven't you? Both having a good laugh."

"Here, steady on." Hugh hovered nervously behind Jenny. "Are you OK, Georgina?"

"She's OK," Jenny sneered. "She can look after herself. She's got a rich bloke in tow, hasn't she? She's fooling him too. Well, I'll stop your little game. You wait and see."

"What the bloody hell's going on here?" Pete was standing in the doorway.

"You two, get your arses into the Starlight Lounge. You're supposed to be on coffee duty. Miss Murphy, are you pissed?"

Georgina shook her head.

"Then get up, get changed, get working. Campbell, get out. Jenny..."

"Get stuffed." Jenny flounced out of the cabin, leaving Pete, although furious at having his authority flouted, unsuccessfully trying to suppress his laughter.

He turned quickly on his heel and left the cabin, leaving Georgina and Hugh together.

"Where is she Georgina?" he asked quietly.

Georgina stared at him. "Why? Why do you want to know?"

"I want to see her, Georgina. I have a right to see her."

"No," Georgina replied, fearfully. "You gave up any right to her when you told me to have an abortion. Anyway, she - might not be yours. I - slept with - someone else."

Georgina was becoming desperate.

"Don't lie, Georgina."

"Hugh. Please. Leave us alone."

"I'll find her, Georgina. I want to see her." His tone was menacing, but Georgina, recognising a threat to her child re-acted like a tigress defending her young. Her voice, thick with emotion, responded fiercely.

"If you come anywhere near her Hugh, I'll kill you."

The Starlight had three days sailing in the North Pacific ahead of her before reaching Honolulu. Most of the passengers were in a good frame of mind, having been helped along by an unscheduled 'Captains gathering' for the people who had been ashore in Los Angeles.

"I hear that the earth moved for all you folk," were his opening words. "Well, lucky you. I wish I'd been there. When we arrive in Honolulu you can ring the folks back home and tell them, quite rightly, how brave you all were. So, the food has arrived and there's plenty of drinks. Go ahead and enjoy."

And this is what they were here for. As much food as they could eat, excellent service, good entertainment and most important, sunshine.

The sun-seekers, were becoming increasingly tanned, the gannets becoming fatter by the hour, all their clothes apparently shrinking, the gamblers grew poorer as the days went by, the spouse seekers had decided on their choice, the social climbers had sussed out who was worth cultivating and the bridge players had routed out the cheats. What they were not aware of was the simmering disquiet and ill-humour that existed between their coffee hostesses.

Pete, having caught up with Jenny had warned her in his inimitable way what would happen to both her and Georgina if any passenger became aware of their antipathy.

"More coffee, madam?" Jenny smiled sweetly at the 'Glums'. "My friend Georgina will bring it for you. Georgina, dear. More coffee over here please. Are you still enjoying the cruise, Mrs Moody?"

"Too hot," grumbled Mrs Moody. "Yes, too hot," repeated Mr Moody.

"Coffee's too strong," complained the woman.

"Always too strong on this ship," agreed her husband.

"Georgina dear. The coffee's too strong. Be a love and go down to the kitchen for a weaker pot, if you don't mind."

Georgina obeyed without question, her independent spirit buried beneath a mound of worry, of despair, of fear. Fear of what Jenny intended to do. She knew that she would take her revenge and Georgina felt that she was entitled to do so. She should have told Jenny immediately she had seen Hugh, just as she should have told Adam about Rosie.

"Whoops, Georgina. You're a thousand miles away, aren't you?"

She'd bumped into Dave on her way to the kitchen. "Oh Dave. What a *mess* I've made of everything."

He placed a finger underneath her chin and lifted her face.

"Hot tears again," he sighed. "Listen, we have rehearsals all day today. See me in the bar tonight and tell Uncle Dave all about it. Have you told Reynolds yet about Rosie?"

Georgina shook her head.

"Well, tell him, for God's sake."

"And what do I say, for God's sake," she retorted sharply, a little of her indomitable spirit returning. "Oh by the way, Adam, I just forgot to mention it, but I had sex at fifteen, had a child at sixteen. The father's a Scottish singer who happens to be on this ship and he's bonking my cabin mate, who doesn't know he's Rosie's father. Well", she continued mournfully, "she didn't, but she does now."

Dave stared at her in disbelief, then whistled.

"Christ, Georgina. You don't do things by half, do you? What did Jenny say?"

Georgina sighed miserably. "She hates me."

Dave gave a short laugh. "I should think that's the understatement of the year. And it's hardly surprising, is it. She'll have it in for you. Anna's got nothing on Jenny if she's crossed. Where are you going now?"

"To the kitchen for coffee. The Glums are moaning."

"So what's new? See you at rehearsals. And Georgina, don't look so... well... *glum.*"

At rehearsals, Jenny was honey sweet to Georgina on the surface, but her thinly veiled barbs didn't go unnoticed by Anna.

"What have you done to her?" she asked Georgina curiously, during a coffee break.

"I've let her down," replied Georgina, quietly. "I've let everyone down. I think I'll go home."

Anna wriggled, uncomfortably. "Aw, don't do that, Look, I know we haven't got on too well." She gave a humourless laugh. "I - don't suppose I get on with anyone really. But I wouldn't want to see you give it up, Georgina. I mean, you're not a bad sort. And you'll never be taken on again if you walk out. Don't let Jenny bother you too much."

Georgina smiled at her, sadly. "Thanks, Anna, but - well - she's entitled."

"Break over, folks. Back to work." The choreographer clapped his hands and motioned to the pianist to start playing.

Georgina's professionalism rose to the surface, the years of firm self discipline and strict training taking over and she concentrated on the intricate steps of a new routine, pleased to be able to put her troubles to the back of her mind. She had decided that this evening, without fail, she would go to Adam's cabin and tell him. She would make or break their relationship.

The choreographer was a hard task master and the dancers worked all day, with only a short stop for lunch. Jenny was now completely ignoring Georgina and Anna had obviously decided to take Georgina under her wing.

"Do you want to change cabins, Georgina? You can share with me."

"No - thanks very much, Anna. I think I should stay where I am."

"Well... if it becomes too difficult you're welcome."

Dave crept up behind her and whispered in her ear. "If it becomes too difficult, George, you can share with me." Georgina laughed at his cheeky remark.

"You're a pal, Dave," she said fervently. "I'll buy you a drink after the show tonight and you can do your agony aunt stuff. See you all later."

Georgina, hoping to see Adam before the show, had gone to his cabin, but he was not in. She pondered as to whether she should leave him a letter. She immediately decided against the idea. This was too important. She needed to see his face, watch his expression to know how he really felt. Needed him to put his arms around her. Tell her at once that he understood and that he still loved her. As Georgina slowly turned away from the cabin door, the door of the next cabin opened. Adam's sister, Eve, stared at her.

"What are you doing here?" she asked icily.

"I - wanted to see Adam - Mr Reynolds."

"Leave my brother alone, do you hear? He can do without the likes of you hanging around him."

The woman's face, twisted with fury, frightened Georgina and without a word, she turned away, hurrying back to the theatre where the show was almost ready to start.

"Where have you been?" whispered Anna. "You'd better get into your costume. The boss's been fuming. You know he insists that we're here fifteen minutes before the show starts."

"She'll have been shagging somewhere, no doubt," sniffed Jenny.

"Pack it in, Jenny," rebuked Dave, sharply.

Georgina changed quickly into the brightly coloured scanty, satin leotard and as she fastened the ostrich plumes on to her head, the band struck up the opening bars of their first number.

Georgina's mind at once switched into automatic drive and she performed, smiling brightly, her eyes seeing no individual in the audience, merely a sea of faces, her adrenalin rising as the show moved forward. Georgina was a true performer, and her ability to achieve mental stability whilst on stage had carried her through many crisis in her young life.

When the show finished, Georgina, still on a high with adrenalin chasing around her body and with the tumultuous applause of an audience ringing in her ears, felt the need to relax before she could face Adam and made her way to the late bar where Dave was waiting for her.

"What do you want to drink, Georgina?"

"My shout," she said. "Beer?"

"Thanks, yes. I've something to tell you. Get the drinks first."

Dave had found a table in a quiet corner and as Georgina placed the drinks on the table, he nudged her.

"I don't want to worry you, but have you seen who Jenny is speaking to?"

Georgina followed Dave's gaze, catching her breath convulsively as she saw Jenny speaking to Eve Reynolds.

"Oh Dave, she's telling her. I know she is. Oh, I must find Adam."

"Georgina, you shoot off and try to find him. I have information for Jenny. I'll try and hold on to her. Stop her before she blows the gaff on you."

The bar was packed, and as Georgina tried to push her way out, she was stopped time after time by passengers wanting to speak to her, to congratulate her on her performance. Normally, she would have been delighted to stop and chat, but now her one thought was to find Adam. Pete, standing with a group of officers, motioned her to join them, but she pretended not to see him. The atmosphere in the bar was humid and she could scarcely breathe. Feeling a breeze drifting in through an open door, Georgina stepped out on to the deck. As she gulped in the fresh Pacific breezes, a figure walked towards her. It was Adam Reynolds. With a deep sigh of relief, she ran towards him.

"What a wonderful performance that was tonight, Georgina. I hardly dare suggest taking you away from your dancing," he smiled.

"Adam," she began urgently. "Can we go to your cabin?"

He held her at arms length, hazel eyes searching her face with amusement.

"What a suggestion! Do you mean to seduce me?"

"Adam, please. I need to speak to you."

They walked to his cabin in silence.

"What is it, Georgina? You're going to tell me you can't give up your career, aren't you? I know I'm asking a lot. All those people out there tonight. You're a consummate entertainer and they just adored you but all their love put together can't match the love I have for you and I know I can make you happy."

As Georgina opened her mouth to speak, the telephone rang.

"Excuse me, darling."

Georgina watched him, fearfully. He listened to his caller in complete silence. Slowly replacing the telephone on its cradle, he turned to her. The tiny muscle in the side of his face twitched. Through tightened lips, he spoke.

"Is it true?"

She knew what he meant. She knew that it had been Eve, telling him about Rosie.

"Answer me, Georgina." His voice was rough and she felt a chill run through her body. "Is it true that you have a child?"

Georgina lowered her eyes, unable to look into his questioning eyes, unable to bear the hurt that she knew she must see.

She nodded, lifting her head now, her eyes pleading, begging him to understand. He half lifted his arms towards her, then lowered them, turning away from her.

"Adam," she whispered helplessly. "Adam - please. Look at me."

"Get out," he said, in a strangled voice.

Georgina remained motionless, shocked. She'd expected him to be angry. To be disappointed in her. But to dismiss her like this was almost more than she could bear.

"Did you hear what I said. Get out of my sight."

She turned to go, then hesitated, and in a tiny, tremulous voice said, "I'll leave the ship when we dock. I'll leave when we get to Honolulu. You won't ever see me again.

Chapter Seven

Georgina slowly undressed, carefully hanging up her clothes. Soon, they would arrive in Honolulu. She could arrange a flight from there. Tomorrow she would tell Pete that she couldn't continue.

She heard foot steps outside and with a sinking heart heard a key turning in the lock. She couldn't bear another session with Jenny. Throwing a robe around her, she stood up, intending to go out and return when Jenny was asleep.

"Don't go, Georgina." Georgina sat down on her bunk and Jenny sat down beside her.

"He's married."

Georgina stared at her in disbelief, "Adam - *married.*"

"No, idiot," replied Jenny, impatiently. "Honestly Georgina. It's me - me-me - with you, isn't it. The world doesn't revolve around you and your piddling little affairs. It's Jock. You know. Your Hugh. Hugh Campbell. The Scottish singer. The Scottish swine. That's why he asked me not to tell anyone he'd asked me to marry him. The bugger already has a wife." Her voice rose sharply. "*And* - he still *lives* with her. If I'd known I'd have stuck his sporran up his arse." She rose from the bunk, looking down on Georgina.

"I'm sorry, kid." Her voice was unusually soft. "I'm really and truly sorry I went on at you. You're the one that's had the heavy end of the stick, having a kid to that bastard. I think we've both had a lucky escape."

"Oh Jenny," gasped Georgina. "I'm so relieved. I've been really worried about you. He can be violent, you know. I kept wanting to warn you."

"Tell you what," Jenny took hold of her hands and pulled her up. "Get dressed. We'll go and celebrate. To hell with all men. Let them see we don't care."

"Oh, Jenny," sighed Georgina. "I don't think I can. I'm not in the mood."

Jenny sat down beside her again, placing her arm around her shoulder.

"Did you sort anything out with Reynolds? George - I've a confession to make. I told Eve Reynolds about Rosie."

Georgina sighed. "I know. She told Adam. She told him before I could."

"Shit," Jenny exploded. "Aw, come on. Let me buy you a drink."

"No, not tonight, Jenny. You go. By the way, how did you find out about Hugh?'

"It was Dave. One of the radio lads asked him to pass a message to Campbell. It was from his wife. All lovey dovey it was. I hope he chokes on his bleeding Haggis. Well, if you're sure you won't come..."

The following morning, whilst Jenny was still sleeping, Georgina went in search of Pete. She knew he was an early riser, often doing a couple of miles walk around the deck before breakfast. Donning a jogging suit, she quietly left the cabin and went outside. The early morning sun struggled to shine, albeit weakly, and she shivered as a cool breeze swept across the almost deserted deck. Leaning on the taffrall at the stern of the ship, she waited. Sure enough Pete came into view.

He stopped when he saw her. "Early bird this morning, aren't you?"

"Pete, can I have a word?"

He gazed at her serious face for a couple of seconds. "Hmm. Let's sit down and have a coffee."

The coffee bar was about to open and Pete motioned to a waiter to bring a pot.

"What is it, Georgina? You got a problem."

The waiter poured out two cups of coffee. Georgina waited until he had gone before speaking.

"I want to come off at Honolulu, Pete. I - can't stay on." Pete stirred his coffee slowly, sipping the hot liquid gratefully. "Ah, wonderful. They make good coffee, don't you think? Georgina, don't be a bloody idiot. Look, I don't go around with my eyes shut. You may not see much of me, but I have my ears close to the ground and I know most of what's going on. It's my job to know. It's Reynolds, isn't it?' Georgina nodded.

"You've a youngster, haven't you?" Georgina looked at him, startled.

"How did..."

"Never mind how I know. Suffice to say that once something's out, it spreads like wildfire on a ship. Georgina - I - don't normally try to persuade anyone to stay. I firmly believe that people will do what they want to do and its no good trying to stop them. But for Christ's sake stop and think, will you? I know being at sea for long periods has its disadvantages, but it's a good job, financially. I've a daughter - Mandy - and I know how much it costs to keep her. If you break your contract, you won't get another chance. Apart from that, you're a good dancer, good hostess. Passengers like you, even the Glums." Georgina looked surprised.

"Yes - I've had some excellent reports on you. I don't want to lose you but - we arrive in Honolulu soon. If you really want to go home, I'll arrange a flight. Think it over and let me know.'

She was still sitting in the coffee bar when Jenny and Dave appeared.

Jenny sat down beside her. "You were up early. What are you up to? Dave, fetch some croissants for us, there's a love."

"I'm thinking of going home. Pete says he'll arrange a flight if I decide to go."

"You're crazy. Give up a job, just for a fella. Listen, so you've lost Reynolds. You didn't have him when you arrived, did you? You were happy enough then. So what's different? And you've had some good times. Bit of rumpy pumpy. Grow up, Georgina."

Dave returned with a dish of croissants. "You're wanted in the board room, Georgina."

"That'll be Pete. Tell him you're staying. Put the dish down Dave and stop gawping. "Go *on*, George."

Georgina made her way slowly to the boardroom. Pete wasn't giving her much time. She knocked on the door. There was no reply. Carefully, she opened the door. A man was standing looking out of the porthole. Georgina caught her breath. It was Adam Reynolds. Her heart began to beat wildly. Everything was going to be alright. That's why he had sent for her. But when he turned to face her, his eyes were cold, his face taut.

"I understand, Miss Murphy, that you are thinking of leaving the ship at Honolulu. That won't be necessary. I shall leave and continue my journey to Sydney by plane."

"Adam," she whispered. "Please - let me explain."

"No need, my dear, I understand perfectly. I thought you were different. You're no better than the rest. You came to my cabin that first night, not because you loved me. You came to get me to *fuck."*

Georgina recoiled as he spat the word at her. She knew that his intention was to insult her, to humiliate her.

"You came looking for a meal ticket," he continued vehemently. "In a couple of weeks, you would have come crying that you're pregnant." He took an envelope out of his packet and threw it on the table. "That should pay for your services."

He strode out of the room, leaving Georgina stunned. For a while, she didn't move. Slowly, what he had said to her began to register and she was filled with a fury that shook her to the very core of her being. How *dare* he speak to her like that. Her first impression of him in the garage had been justified. He was a hateful, arrogant man, with an inflated ego. She trembled with rage. Rage and indignation, both at him and his sister.

She made up her mind. Yes, she was going to stay on this ship. Let Reynolds fly off to Sydney if that's what he wanted to do. Good riddance! But she would seek out Eve Reynolds. She would teach her a lesson. She would tell her exactly what she thought of her. She'd been the cause of all this. By this time, Georgina was beyond constructive reasoning. She wanted to lash out, to hurt, as he had hurt her.

Turning sharply on her heels, Georgina left the boardroom to seek out Pete. To tell him that she would be staying to complete the cruise. Picking up the envelope, she walked down to the purser's desk and handed it to the assistant purser.

"Would you make sure Mr. Reynolds receives this, please."

The young man smiled and nodded. "Will do," he said cheerfully. "Are you looking forward to Honolulu, Georgina?"

She was surprised that he knew her name, then she realised that a ship is a tiny community. An insular life style. And she was now part of it, with friends and companions. She'd be crazy to give it all up. Jenny was right. She'd been elated when she had been appointed to this job. Why should she destroy it for a man? A man who was not worth it. She was confident too that Robert Barnes, the company's Head of Entertainment, wouldn't sack her now that they were half way through the cruise. She was doing a good job. Pete had said so.

She smiled at the young man. "Yes. Yes, I am. I've never been to Honolulu before."

"A crowd of us are going to Waikiki Beach. If you want to join us you're welcome. Meet here as soon as we have clearance to go ashore."

"Thanks. Thanks ever so much. I might take you up on that."

She hummed to herself as she made her way back to the coffee bar. She didn't need Adam Reynolds, she told herself defiantly. Plenty of men would be happy to be in her company.

Jenny and Dave had already gone by the time she returned, but Pete was sitting having breakfast. The sight of his plate of bacon and egg reminded Georgina that she hadn't eaten.

"Mind if I join you, Pete?"

"Not at all, grab a seat."

"Pete, I'd like to stay."

Pete nodded. "I should think so too. I told Reynolds I didn't want to lose you. That you needed the work."

"Oh Pete, you *didn't.*"

"It's true, isn't it? Georgina, it's a harsh world, as you must have found out. I don't know what went wrong between you two, but its nothing to him to fly from Honolulu to Sydney. He's loaded. And if it gets him out of your hair and it means I don't lose you, then he can go. As it happens, it probably suits him to go. Get away from his sister for a while. Must go."

Georgina was confused. From the way Adam Reynolds had spoken to her, he wasn't in the mood to be doing her any favours. And yet, why should he leave the way clear for her to stay on board. However, it was a small part of her life that she was determined to put behind her. She intended concentrating on her work now and enjoying the trips ashore. She would ask Dave if he wanted to join the crowd on Waikiki Beach. Perhaps Jenny would come too, And - she decided she would ask Anna. In fact, Georgina was feeling incredibly magnanimous. She'd even decided that perhaps Eve Reynolds was not worth bothering about.

There was a giggle and a squeal from the swimming pool and Georgina turned in time to see Adam Reynolds throw the 'nympho' into the water. Their eyes met briefly, and for a second Georgina was sure that she caught a glimpse of tenderness. He turned away from her abruptly, following the woman into the pool. Grabbing hold of her, he pulled her under the water and Georgina watched as Adam drew her to him, kissing her passionately.

Georgina pushed back her chair noisily and, with hot tears stinging her eyes, she left the scene. How could she have thought that she didn't need him. The sight of his lean, tanned body that she had such intimate knowledge of, his strong arms that had held her so lovingly, filled her with such a burning desire, she felt faint.

Leaning against the rail of the ship, she closed her eyes, reliving their first real kiss. Not the brief, unexpected kiss in the garage, but a long, hot, searching kiss that had left both of them reeling with delight in anticipation of the sexual pleasures which were inevitably to follow.

"Miss Murphy."

Gasping, she turned around. "Adam," she whispered.

He stood beside her, wrapped in a towelling robe. Half lifting her arms, she looked up at him, anxiously searching for some small sign that he still wanted her, but his face was a blank mask.

"You returned the money." His voice was expressionless. "Are you - alright? "

Georgina's arms dropped limply to her side. "You mean, am 1 likely to be pregnant," she replied, sarcastically. "Well, if I am, I'm sure I`ll be able to cope. After all, I've done it before. You'd better return to your - to her.'

His brown eyes flashed into life and his lips tightened.

"She's honest. I know where I am with her. I - leave when we reach Honolulu. I don't suppose we shall meet again."

"No" replied Georgina coldly. "I don't suppose we will."

She turned away from him, gazing out over the seemingly endless expanse of water, glinting bright blue and pearly green, where the now strong sunlight caught the rise and fall of the swell. She felt his presence with her for several seconds, but she remained still, giving no indication that she was aware of him. When Georgina eventually turned, he was gone.

"Dave, Jenny, anything planned for tomorrow?"

Georgina leaned on her elbow, squinting in the sun as they all took a welcome break around the swimming pool.

"I see we're all friends again." Anna spread out a large bath towel and lay flat on her back, tipping her sunhat over her eyes.

"What are you thinking of doing, Georgina?" asked Dave.

"Waikiki Beach. There's a crowd meeting at the purser's desk. Anna, do come with us."

Anna yawned and sat up. 'That's child's play. I'm going shopping."

"Are you going to the Ala Moana Centre?" Jenny asked, eagerly. "If you are, I'll come with you."

"OK." She lay down again, covering her face once more. "We'll buy a grass skirt for Georgina's little bastard."

Georgina bit her lip, determined not to fall out with anyone. Now that she and Jenny were speaking, Anna's period of good will was over, her bitter mind working overtime again.

Glancing at Dave, Georgina smiled her thanks as he placed his finger on his lips, willing her not to rise to Anna's bait.

"What's the Ala Moana?" asked Georgina.

Jenny sat up, sharply. "What's the Ala Moana? Don't you know? It's only one of the largest shopping centres in the world. You can buy absolutely everything there."

"Georgina, don't go with the crowd. I'll plan a day for us. We'll go to the beach as early as we can, before it's too hot then we'll do other things. I think you should see Pearl Harbour, Georgina and if we've got time, we could go to the zoo and then..."

"Hey, stop there,"laughed Georgina. "I think that'll be enough."

"Yea, I suppose it will. I'm going for a swim."

Dave jumped into the pool, followed by the three girls.

The quayside was a panorama of brilliant colour, lined with stands which were filled with local works of art. The ground, a kaleidoscope of flowers, was constantly changing and being replaced as garlands were placed around the necks of passengers as they stepped off the gangway.

The Hawaiians are great lovers of flowers and the 'Lei', the garland, comprised of carnations, crown flowers and plumeria, is a symbol of friendship. A steel band had welcomed the Starlight into the Honolulu harbour and now the 'Hula' was being performed by dancers, young and old, all smiling happily, pleased to entertain the visitors who would soon be spending and contributing towards the economy of the Hawaiian Islands.

Passengers, of course, had priority in disembarking, all anxious to see as much as possible in the short time they would be in dock. The crew and staff who were lucky enough to have time off hovered impatiently in the background, awaiting their turn to leave the ship.

At the exit stood a large blackboard informing everyone of the time of departure and if anyone arrived back too late, that was unfortunate. The ship waited for no-one.

Dave and Georgina stood on the deck watching passengers eagerly stepping on to land. Lines of taxis were in waiting, all hopeful of securing a good fare, and as many of the passengers were elderly, their long wait was often rewarded with a full days booking.

"Georgina, is that Reynolds? He's got a couple of cases with him."

"Yes," Georgina replied, slowly. "Didn't you know. He's left the ship. He's flying to Sydney."

Adam Reynolds was standing with his sister. He looked in Georgina's direction. They were too far apart for her to read anything in his expression and she was able to watch him without feeling uncomfortable. His dark hair glinted in the sun and as he shaded his eyes with his hand from the glare, she recalled how those long, sensitive fingers had caressed her, how he had run them through her hair and over her face. How they had touched her limbs with tenderness, holding her tightly as their mutual passion had grown.

She knew that Dave was watching her carefully and turned away from the quayside.

"What happened, Georgina? Why is he going?"

"I - didn't get the chance to tell him about Rosie myself, Dave. Eve Reynolds did that for me."

"The bitch."

"No Dave. She's his sister, after all. I suppose she was protecting him from - a gold-digger." Her voice wavered and Dave swore.

"He was horrible to me, Dave. I honestly meant to tell him. I didn't set out to lie to anyone. It - just happened."

"Then he's a fool." Dave's voice was thick with emotion. "I wish you could love me, Georgina. I'd look after you. And Rosie." Georgina kissed him and as she did, she saw Adam Reynolds turn away quickly and, climbing into a taxi, drive away towards the airport.

With a quivering sigh, Georgina smiled weakly at Dave. "End of an unfortunate episode. I think we can go ashore now."

They gathered their bags and made their way down to the exit and out on to the quay. Georgina began to wander amongst the merchandise laid out on the stands and on the ground.

Dave pulled her back. "Don't buy anything now," he whispered. "Wait till the ships ready to sail. You'll be able to buy things cheaper. Come on. Let's grab a taxi to the beach. We'll spend a couple of hours there."

Georgina was beginning to realise that Dave had been wise to insist on going to the beach early in the morning. By eleven, the heat was almost overwhelming, and Georgina was relieved when Dave suggested that they move on.

"Where next, my intrepid guide. I'm completely in your hands."

"Oh, Georgie, how I wish you were," sighed Dave, mournfully.

Georgina laughed at his expression. "Come on, Dave. You don't really mean that. I wonder how many times you've been in and out of love on these trips."

"Once or twice," he admitted, ruefully. "Well," as she looked at him quizzically, "perhaps three or four."

"You're a great guy, Dave. You'll meet a super girl one of these days, not a shop soiled one like me."

"Don't say that, Georgina," said Dave, earnestly. "Is that how Reynolds made you feel?"

She nodded, and the hot tears, never far away these days it seemed, brimmed over.

"He's hurt you, hasn't he?" He was angry now.

Georgina brushed away her tears, impatiently. "Oh, I'm sorry, Dave. It's all over now. Where are you taking me? "

"Well," responded Dave, enthusiastically. "My treat, cos you've been a pal. We are going on - wait for it - The ATLANTIS SUBMARINE. We're going under the water to see another world, and then we'll go to Pearl Harbour and on to..."

"OK boss. Lead on."

Excitedly, they boarded the sleek catamaran which was to take them the short distance to the dive site, about a mile off-shore and within minutes of boarding the Atlantis, they were in an aquarium in reverse, with a breath-taking view of an underwater world, swarming with marine life. The under-water vessel was cool, with air conditioned temperature, a pleasant relief from the sun baked beach of Waikiki. The pair of them delighted at the sight of tropical fish pressing their mouths to the portholes. The trip finished with a tour of the Waikiki coastline.

"Lunch, I think. My treat Dave, and I insist," as he opened his mouth to protest.

He smiled. "You're an independent miss, aren't you? So where are you taking me?"

"Don't know," laughed Georgina. "You choose."

Dave assumed a pseudo French accent. "I weel tek you, ma cherie, to a leetle French cafe called Michel's. We weel dine off ze oysters, which is ze aphrodisiac."

"Oooh, can't wait."

Hand in hand, they ran to find Michel's, where they had a superb French meal, declined the oysters, both of them deciding that if the old adage was true, in their case it would be a waste of money.

"You don't have to come if you don't want, Georgina." Dave was desperate to visit Pearl Harbour.

"Well, if you don't mind, Dave, I think I'd like to do some shopping."

Dave was doubtful. "I shouldn't let you go on your own."

Georgina smiled. "I'm a big girl. I'll be alright. I'll go to the... what was it... the Ala Moana. I'll probably see Jenny and Anna there. You go on, Dave. I'll see you back on board."

"Well - if you're sure, we'll take a taxi. You can drop off at the shopping centre. It's on the way. I'd come with you only I've been loads of times. It's a great place, Georgina. Huge. About fifty acres, if you can imagine that. Nearly two hundred stores. Lots of speciality shops and good restaurants. Don't go spending all your money though. I tell you, it's hard to resist buying and buying. Just wait till you see what Anna and Jenny come back with."

Georgina soon found that Dave was right about spending money. The Ala Moana was an invitation to shop till you drop. But Georgina was cautious and contented herself with window shopping although, after some hesitation, she treated herself to a lovely corn blue silk shirt, ignoring Jenny's advice. "Wait till we go to Hong Kong before you buy any silks."

It was only after she left the shop that she admitted to herself that the reason she'd bought it was because it was the same colour as the flowers that had been on the table the night she had dined in Adam's cabin.

Back on the Starlight, the decks were deserted, passengers eager to see as much as possible of Honolulu. Young stewards wandered around aimlessly, just for once having little to do. Georgina leaned on the rails, trying to interest herself in the activities that take place when a great liner is preparing to sail. Fresh provisions had already been taken on board and taxis were starting to arrive on the quayside, bringing passengers back to the ship ready for the next leg of their journey.

But Georgina's thoughts were elsewhere, with a tall, dark-haired guy who's piercing eyes had held hers in an almost hypnotic trance. Whose strong arms had held her so close. Whose lips had kissed hers with a demanding passion. Yet after all passion was spent had kissed her so tenderly and caringly she had cried. Had he really forgotten all that? Could he really hate her so much?

"Miss." One of the stewards waved to her, motioning that someone on the quayside was trying to catch her attention.

She caught her breath. "Adam", she breathed, frantically searching amongst the gathering crowds.

But it wasn't Adam Reynolds. Hugh Campbell, about to climb into a taxi, waved to her.

He cupped his hands to his mouth and shouted. "I'll find her, Georgina. I'll find her."

Georgina turned away from the rails, icy fingers gripping her heart. Half forgotten memories came flooding back, swirling around her mind like a vulture over its prey. When Hugh Campbell was sober, he appeared gentle and caring. But when he'd been drinking, he could be vicious and obsessive. If, in one of these moods, he decided he wanted to find Rosie, he would move heaven and earth to do so. And having now finished his stint of entertaining on the Starlight, he was on his way back to England. What would he do if he found her? She had to phone her mum. She must warn her that Hugh Campbell was going to be searching for them.

Chapter Eight

Georgina awoke early the following morning. Jenny was still sleeping and Georgina turned on to her back and stretched out her arms, moving quietly so as not to disturb her cabin-mate. There was barely a movement from the Starlight as she sailed smoothly and tranquilly towards the Samoan Island of Tutuila. Her fear of Hugh Campbell finding Rosie had disappeared. She felt she'd panicked unnecessarily. He'd no idea where Rosie lived. And if he did find her, she'd every confidence in her mum. She knew she would never let Rosie out of her sight. And as for the other bloke, Reynolds, Jenny was right. He was history. She was going to concentrate on her work and enjoy the rest of the cruise.

"Morning girls." The smiling steward placed a tray on the table. "You visit Pango-Pango today?"

Jenny, now wide awake, sat up in her bunk.

"Yea, soon as we can."

"You know girls, you must be very careful. The people here are very modest in the town so don't wear any swim suits, only on the beach. And you mustn't stretch your legs out when you sit down and no eating when you walk through a village."

Jenny nodded. "You're right. I've been before. But the folks here are lovely. Really friendly."

Georgina looked inquiringly at the steward. "I thought the capital was Pago-Pago."

"Pango-Pango is the old name."

"Hang on. You're new. Where's our old steward?" Jenny sipped her tea, adding quickly, "but this is very good tea."

"I was Mr Reynolds' steward. He asked for me to be your steward. Have a good day."

Georgina gasped. "Oh Jenny. Did you hear that. I think Adam wants to make sure I'm OK. I think he still loves me."

Jenny almost choked on her tea. "I don't believe you. *He never* loved you. Can't you *see* that. You were a bit of nookie on what would have been for him a very boring trip. He'll have done this cruise hundreds of times. I'll tell you what he's done. He'll have paid that lad to keep an eye on you. Count the number of bonking sessions going on. Ease what bit of conscience he might have. Come on, George. Let's go to the retreat for a couple of hours and do a spot of sun-bathing. It'll take that long for the passengers to go ashore. I bags the first shower."

Georgina remained silent but inside her indignation was starting to rise. Jenny could be right. How could she have been so stupid to think that Reynolds still cared for her?

Dave and Anna were already installed on loungers when they arrived at the retreat.

"Dave, fill George in on Pago-Pago. Take her mind of that bastard Reynolds. Do you know what he's done now?"

"Jenny, *please*" entreated Georgina. "Leave it. But yes, Dave. I do want to know about these islands."

"Oh *no.*" moaned Anna . "Not *another* geography lesson."

"Hey smart arse. Perhaps if you listened sometimes, you wouldn't be such an ignoramus," snapped Jenny. "Go on, Dave."

Dave needed no encouragement to air his knowledge and assuming his teacher stance began. "There were lots of escaped convicts and runaway sailors settled on the islands which is why they were followed by missionaries from London so, they're a very religious people."

"Oh, that's boring, Dave." Jenny looked up from filing her nails. "Broke a bloody nail yesterday. What about the shops? That's what George wants to know. George, we'll go on one of the buses, well, converted trucks to one of the markets. They're beautifully painted. You'll love them. Bit of a bumpy ride though. Anyway, you can buy baskets and bags and even mats, all woven from leaves."

"Sounds great," smiled Georgina. "Anything else to tell me, Dave?"

"Well, er... it has an annual rain-fall of two hundred inches."

"Fascinating." mocked Anna.

Dave ignored her, continuing "There's a building here called the 'old boarding house', made famous by some writer..."

"Somerset Maugham's story of Sadie Thompson. It's called 'Rain.'

Anna stood up and, ever conscious of the lustful stares of young officers, adjusted her shorts and, slim hips swaying provocatively, walked away from them.

Georgina burst out laughing at the look of astonishment on Jenny's face.

"How did she know..."

Dave interjected. "Egg on your face, Jenny. She's hardly an ignoramus.

First class honours degree in English. Didn't you know?"

The Starlight had ten days sailing ahead of her before reaching New Zealand and now everyone was looking forward to crossing the equator.

"It's good fun," Jenny admitted. "I've done it many times, but I have to admit, I always enjoy it. Even the old man joins in."

"You mean the Captain?" asked Georgina, in a surprised voice.

"Mm. He's a good sport. Most of the Captains are very sociable, you know. I suppose it's part of the job, mixing with the hoi polloi. And no matter how often they do the crossing ceremony, you'd think it was the first time for everyone. You see, for most people, a cruise is a one off, and really, we all try to make it good for them."

Georgina was puzzled. Jenny, normally so cynical, was in an extremely generous frame of mind.

"Jenny - don't yell at me, but you have got over Hugh - Jock, haven't you?"

"Who?" Jenny answered in an icy tone, making it obvious that she didn't intend speaking of her ex-lover.

Georgina, taking the hint, changed the subject. "Hey, we've been so busy lately, I forgot to ask if you bought anything in Honolulu."

The girls were sitting in their cabin listening to the radio.

"Certainly did."

She opened one of her drawers and handed Georgina a bag.

Georgina looked at it questioningly. "What is it?"

"Go *on*. Have a look."

Georgina dived inside the bag and with a squeal of delight, brought out a tiny grass skirt, a cotton top and a garland made of feathers.

Jenny beamed at her pleasure. "It's for Rosie. From Anna and me."

"Thank you, Jenny. That's very kind of you. But - why Anna? I mean - she can be so - well - you know what I mean."

"She can be a bloody bitch," agreed Jenny. "She's a strange girl, yet sometimes she's bearable. It was her idea to buy it."

The radio stopped playing music.

"Message coming up, George."

The two girls were silent.

"Man over board. Man overboard. Lower the lifeboats. Lower the lifeboats."

Georgina felt her blood run cold. "Jenny," she whispered, her voice shaking with horror. "What do we do?"

"Well, unless you fancy jumping in - sod all," replied Jenny, dryly.

Georgina was horrified at her cabin mate's lack of concern, and grabbing hold of her arm, yelled frantically, "Come *on.* We must go and see."

Jenny sighed. "Ah well. If we must."

Georgina had now been at sea long enough to know that, no matter what the circumstances were, one did not run anywhere on a ship, and together, they dutifully walked quickly along the gangway, up the stairs and out on to the stern deck of the ship. There were a number of passengers leaning over the rail, pointing their fingers into the distance.

"Jenny," gasped Georgina. "This is *awful.* Oh, I wonder who it is?" Her thoughts flew immediately to Adam. What if... ? She gave herself a shake. Adam wasn't even on the Starlight. She must stop thinking about him. He'd gone and she would never see him again. The kind of people he mixed with meant that they were poles apart.

Jenny shrugged her shoulders. "Who ever it is, George, they'll probably have been eaten by sharks by now."

Georgina shuddered. "There's Dave. I'll see if he knows anything."

Jenny leaned on the rail, watching Georgina with an amused expression on her face and when she returned, burst out laughing.

"You *knew* didn't you?" Georgina's face was red.

"I'm sorry, George. I couldn't resist that. They do this exercise two or three times during the cruise. Actually, it's quite interesting. They take the ship in a figure eight, so that it comes back to where the person fell overboard. It's called the Williamson Turn. There, look. They've picked up the dummy."

A cheer went up from the watching crowd and the Starlight was very quickly back on course for the equator.

The following days passed uneventfully. Georgina, now well used to the daily routine and the arduous rehearsals, was able to take the long hours in her stride. She was very rarely in bed before one in the morning and up again at seven. She tried to keep herself busy most of the time, throwing herself into her work with enthusiasm and vigour, which delighted Pete and the choreographer, but often left Jenny gasping.

"Christ, Georgina. Slow down, will you. Pete will expect all of us to work at your pace."

"I need to work, Jenny. If I don't, I think about him. It's no good. I try to stay furious with him, but I can't."

"Can't you cast your eyes elsewhere? You could practically take your pick amongst the fellows."

"Even Vince, the handsome officer?' asked Georgina, mischievously.

Jenny's eyes narrowed. "Don't you..." She caught the laughter in Georgina's eyes and relaxed.

"Yes - it's on again with me and him. Well - no good crying over spilt milk, is it? Jock led me up the garden path, good and proper. *Me* - with all my experience. Tell you, girl, you'd no chance. Was he married when you and him were at it?'

"I - don't think so Jenny. He begged me to marry him, but... well - I wasn't quite sixteen when I fell pregnant."

"Did you never think of getting rid?"

"No - never. And when I look at Rosie now, I was right, wasn't I?"

Jenny picked up the child's photograph and stared at it, silently.

"Yes," she said softly. "You were right, Georgina." She leaned over and kissed her cheek. "You were a brick, though. I couldn't have done it."

"Well, my mum was great. I don't suppose I could have done it without her."

Jenny sighed. "You know, I still feel dreadful about, you know, telling Eve Reynolds. If you'd had the chance to tell him yourself, it might have worked out. I feel it was all my fault."

Georgina shook her head. "I should have told him at the beginning."

"Did you know that Robert Barnes is coming on at New Zealand?"
Georgina shuddered as she remembered the cold, calculating eyes of the man who had interviewed her.

"No - I didn't. Why is he coming on?"

Jenny shrugged. "He often does, on a world cruise. Check up on all of us, I suppose. And probably to have a cosy chat with Eve Reynolds."

Georgina sat pensively for a while. "Do you think she'll tell him about me?"

"Bound to, isn't she? But the way you've worked, I wouldn't worry too much. Pete thinks you're the cat's whiskers these days."

"I'm not trying to - you know - curry favours," said Georgina anxiously. "You don't think that, do you, Jenny?"

"Course not. Hey, it's time we were showered. Nearly time for the show."

The Starlight was expected to cross the Equator around four pm. Jenny was right. There was an air of excitement throughout the ship. Everyone, from the Captain down to the humblest seaman, threw themselves into the festivities with gay abandon. A canvas pool was being built on the stern deck into which would be thrown anyone who would offer themselves, on condition that it was their first crossing.

Pete's people were to be very involved in the activities and at the meeting that morning, Georgina had been most impressed by the serious manner in which the proceedings were approached. The air of professionalism of all concerned was a joy to see, and Georgina felt a surge of pride at being part of the scene.

Everyone was thoroughly briefed, even the Captain. This was Pete's show and all authority was invested in him on this occasion. The safety officers would be in position and if anything went wrong, all personnel knew that, at the sound of their signal, everything must stop. When at sea, discipline is, and must be seen to be, absolute.

King Neptune was chosen, and his wife, the surgeon, executor and the bell boy. Georgina was picked for this role, having been warned that she must expect to be thrown into the pool. When Pete was finally satisfied that everyone knew exactly what had to be done, he dismissed them with a last order.

"All pray for a dry afternoon."

"What happens if it rains, Dave?"

"We cancel."

"After all these preparations have been made?`

"Yup. Safety always comes first, Georgina. They have electrical equipment on deck. If it rains, it could be dangerous and the decks would be slippery. No one takes any chances on a ship. Remember, we're a long way from land and there's a lot of water out there. It's easy to become a bit blasé when you've been on a ship for a while, but you should always respect the sea."

Georgina was thoughtful. Dave was right. She'd long since ceased to worry about all that water beneath her, but suddenly, she thought about poor old Mrs Riley, buried at sea. A cold shiver ran through her. And she wanted Adam. She wanted to feel his arms around her. Strong arms, keeping her safe and warm. She wanted to lie in his bed, their limbs entwined, his mouth seeking hers, his sensitive fingers running over her, rousing her passion to match his. She loved him. He was the love of her life. No one else would do. And she'd lost him. Dave touched her arm and she turned to him, burying her head on his chest.

He stroked her hair gently. "Georgina, forget him. He's gone. It's finished. Can't you love me, Georgina? Just a little."

She lifted her head to look at him "What - now?' she asked anxiously.

In spite of himself, Dave laughed. “No, Georgina. Not now. Not this very minute. How about coming to my cabin tonight.” He stroked the hair back from her forehead. “Please?”

Georgina thought about it for a few minutes and was tempted. It would be so good to relax in someone’s arms and be loved. And then she remembered the night in Adam’s cabin and she sighed.

“It’s no good, Dave. I can’t. Even if I never see him again, I don’t think I could ever love another man.”

The weather remained fine and very, very hot. The crossing the line ceremony had passed of extremely well. Neptune had gone back to the deep together with all his courtiers, intrepid passengers had been shaved, covered in gunge and dipped in the pool.

The bell boy, Georgina, had performed admirably and it was now left to the crew from ‘below stairs’ to clear away which they did with incredible speed. Soon, everything was ‘ship shape and Bristol fashion’.

Elderly, exhausted passengers made their way into the restaurant for cream teas, many of the ones who had cruised in the old days insisting that ‘it wasn’t done like it used to be’.

Jenny, overhearing these remarks vowed darkly that, “If it was left to me, I’d dip them in the bleeding Pacific and let Neptune look after them.”

Both Jenny and Georgina were in charge of that days Bingo session and after a quick hose down by a delighted seaman, they changed back into uniform and made their way to the Starlight Lounge, where the Bingo players were waiting for them.

That night, Pete let his team go off duty at midnight and Jenny and Georgina gratefully stumbled wearily to their cabin, taking a gin and tonic each with them.

“Let’s go to bed, George and have our drink in comfort.”

They undressed quickly and climbed into their respective bunks.

“Ah, bliss. An early night and a gin. What more could a girl want,” breathed Jenny.

“Jenny... can I ask you something?”

“Mmm. Make it quick. I’m nearly asleep.”

“I nearly went to bed with Dave today.”

Jenny, almost choking on her drink, gasped.“What do you mean - nearly?”

“Jenny - you don’t think I’m turning into a nympho, do you? I mean - first

Hugh, then Adam - and now Dave. I had just been telling myself of my undying love for Adam Reynolds and suddenly - I wanted to go to bed with Dave. Do you think it's something to do with being at sea? Perhaps it's the sea air. Jenny - are you asleep?"

Georgina raised herself to look into the top bunk. Jenny was shaking with suppressed mirth, and when she saw Georgina's face peeping at her, she dissolved into peals of laughter. Georgina, after a few seconds of hurt silence, joined in.

Jenny sat up and, swinging her long legs out of her bunk, sat down beside her cabin mate, placing an arm around her shoulder.

"Listen, you're no different to the rest of us, except Anna. She's a dark horse. I've never been able to work her out. And with her qualifications should she be in this job? Mebbe she's been badly hurt along the way. She's a bit of a tease with the blokes but - well - that can be a dangerous game. I've never known her to be really involved with any guy even though she often says she fancies a particular bloke from time to time. Like she said she fancied Reynolds. But nothing ever seems to happen. Maybe she's a lesbian. I don't know. Anyway, the rest of us, I suppose, are just looking for a bit of comfort in an alien world. It's not natural, is it, to be floating around in this bloody great container? And it's difficult to sort out true feelings when we're all thrown together the way we are here. Not much choice, you see. So we take what we can, while we can. Some of the fellows I fancy, I wouldn't give them a second glance if I met them on shore. If I'd have met Campbell on land, I'd have seen through him and I wouldn't have wanted Vince, even though he is a big boy, if you know what I mean. And - he never asked me to marry him, cos he told me straight away he was married. So it's all above board see. Not like that creep, Campbell."

"Are you not bothered about his wife?" asked Georgina curiously.

"Well, he's not so I don't see why I should be. She should be grateful to me really. I keep him faithful while we're afloat. He doesn't mess around with anyone else but me."

Georgina sat musing for a little while, trying to work out Jenny's logic.

"Dave's a good looking lad." Jenny continued. "There's nothing wicked in your having wanted to shag him. But you didn't - and that's the difference between you and the nympho."

"Adam was kissing her in the swimming pool."

"Did he know you could see him?"

“I think so,“ nodded Georgina.

Jenny smiled knowingly as she climbed back into her own bunk. “I think you were right not to shag Dave. Save yourself, George. Anyway, Dave’s not all that good in bed.”

Chapter Nine

"What shall we do in Auckland? Any plans anyone?"
Dave, smoothing suntan lotion on his long legs, looked questioningly at Jenny and Georgina. After Georgina had turned down his invitation to a night of passion in his cabin, Dave had maintained a hurt dignity for a couple of days, treating Georgina coolly. He was, however, too good natured to sulk for long, and to Georgina's relief, had sought her out one night in the bar to buy her a drink.

"I've no plans." Jenny stretched out her longs legs with cat-like grace on the lounger at the side of the swimming pool. "Vince is on duty, so I'm free."

"I suppose we shall all have our usual grilling from fart-face." Anna joined the three, slipping off a robe to reveal a tiny, brilliant white bikini, which showed off her golden tan to perfection.

Dave whistled. "Christ, Anna. Where did you buy that from?"
Jenny, removing her sunglasses to inspect the two minute pieces of cloth, sniffed.

"From the childrens' department I would think."

Anna ran her hands over her stomach. "At least, I don't have any stretch marks."

Although Georgina's skin was as smooth as Anna's, she was aware of the innuendo, but was unperturbed by the remark. She was learning to take the cut and thrust in her stride, ignoring anything that could be hurtful with ease, and parrying the innocuous attacks with equal sting.

"What are you intending doing, Anna?" Anna looked embarrassed at Georgina's friendly tone. "Perhaps we could all go out together. You old timers can show me round. Who's 'fart-face?" she asked as an afterthought.

"Robert Barnes," interjected Jenny. "I told you. He's flying in to join us for a couple of weeks."

"He's a shrewd old sod. Watch your step, Georgina." Anna jumped into the swimming pool and swam around lazily.

Jenny shook her head. "She's an odd ball, that one. I don't know what makes her tick. One minute she's cruel, next minute she'd do anything for you."

"Hey, land ahoy." Dave stood up, shading his eyes from the blazing sun. The girls joined him, scanning the horizon. After ten days sailing, the sight of land created excitement in everyone.

"We should be there in a couple of hours. Let's all go out for a meal when we dock. Agreed?"

The girls nodded. "Agreed."

Georgina arrived back on board exhausted. Dave, with his usual enthusiastic drive had certainly shown her Auckland, starting with a drive through the city centre, past Auckland's University and the famous Parnell Bridge, arriving at the summit of Mt Eden, where they had a panoramic view of the city. Jenny and Anna had decided they would rather shop, Jenny being on the look out for Maori carvings and Anna determined to buy greenstone and silver jewellery. The four of them had arranged to meet for an early evening meal, Dave being desperate for new Zealand lamb, which he swore was the best in the world. Anna said she was dying for a Pavlova and Jenny decided she was fed-up eating healthily and would order a Kiwi Burger.

"Which is?" asked Georgina.

"A massive meat patty topped with egg and beetroot."

Anna shuddered delicately. "How absolutely revolting."

All of them had sampled the inexpensive green-lipped mussels, turning down Dave's suggestion that the Auckland rock oyster would do them all a power of good.

After the meal, they finished the day with a visit to the World Expo Pavilion, a building moved from Brisbane after World Expo 88 and then gazed in wonder at the giant waterfall and a bush entrance featuring Kauri trees.

Jenny, throwing off her shoes, flung herself on to Georgina's bunk.

"I begin to understand why some of these passengers say that port calls interfere with cruising. I'm completely knackered. Think I'll give Vince a miss tonight."

"Jenny, I'm really worried about Robert Barnes. What do you think he'll say about Rosie? Eve Reynold's sure to tell him."

"You're worrying unnecessarily. But... if you'd told him at the outset, none of this would have happened and you might still have had Reynolds. The company's not *so* moral. It's just that they like to have your undivided attention. Let's shower, tart ourselves up and go for a drink."

There were no shows performed on board when the ship was in port and the dancers appreciated the break, although they were still 'on duty' and were expected to circulate with passengers. Georgina and Jenny were joined by the rest of Pete's people and spent a pleasant hour relaxing and exchanging stories.

"Did you know that one of the old dears went to the captain during a storm and asked if he could stop the ship during the night so that she could get a good night's sleep?" "That's nothing. Someone asked me the other day if the crew slept on board."

"And what about the poor sod who goes up and down in the lift all day cos he can't find his cabin?"

"Well, the one I feel most sorry for is the old lady who cries when we finally dock. She says she doesn't want to go home because there's no-one there. And the woman who said she was so glad the sun was shining cos her daughter in Wales was going out for the day. And *we...* were in the middle of the bloody Indian Ocean." "Well, this is my favourite. A couple went to see the doc and the receptionists asks 'Name please?' 'Mr and Mrs Brookes.' Writes it down. 'No s on the end.' Receptionist tears up form and starts again. 'Right, Mrs Brooke. Cabin number?' 'Six floors down.' 'Right. Which deck is that?' 'The ones with the cabins on' Receptionists turn to husband. 'Do you know the cabin number?' He does. 'Now, Mr Brooke. Have you seen the doctor before?' 'Yes. lots of times. 'And, whats your problem? 'Haven't got a problem. 'Then when did you last see the doctor?' 'I see him every night in the bar.' A young officer joined them, saying, "Hey Jenny, remember last year when they sent out that 'activities of the day'? Someone must have been suffering from a hangover or something. At the end of the bulletin, they added 'And now piss off'. The printers never noticed and it went out to every cabin. The old man went spare." "And do you remember...".

Georgina smiled as the stories became increasingly outrageous and, leaning back in her chair she closed her eyes, enjoying the friendly buzz of conversation around her. Outside her own close circle of friends, she was still shy and didn't contribute a great deal to the general conversation. She thought about Jenny's comments that she may still have Adam, if she'd been more open. Perhaps that was true, but on the other hand, he couldn't have really loved her, otherwise he would have accepted Rosie. The thought of her child filled her with a desperate longing to see her and for the first time since she had left, she was homesick. There was such a long way to go yet.

Georgina was awakened from her reverie by a dig in the ribs. Pete was approaching them with a speed that indicated trouble.

"Mingle," he hissed. Everyone except Georgina, apparently, knew why and promptly dispersed.

"Robbie Barnes is on his way," whispered Jenny. "Go find someone to speak to."

Georgina looked around her, trying to spot a familiar face and found herself staring into the pale, lack-lustre eyes of the Entertainments Director.

"Good evening Miss Murphy."

"Go... good evening - sir."

Undecided as to whether she should walk away or wait to be dismissed, she half turned from him.

"I hear from Pete that you have taken well to life at sea. He tells me that you work hard and that he's pleased with you."

"Thank you, sir. I do my best."

"Good - good, keep it up."

He attempted a smile, but it was an expression, as Georgina remembered, he didn't achieve easily, and his eyes remained cold. He walked away, leaving her feeling relieved. Eve Reynolds obviously hadn't spoken to him.

Cheerfully, Georgina approached the Glums. "Did you go ashore today?"

"No. Been before."

"Been before."

Sighing, Georgina resigned herself to a period of melancholia. Half an hour later, even Georgina's natural ability to be attentive wavered, and making a lame excuse, she extricated herself. As she turned away, she saw Robert Barnes speaking to Eve Reynolds. Her heart froze. This was it. She was sure that Eve was going to tell him about Rosie.

Georgina opened her eyes to find Jenny standing beside her with a cup of tea.

"Come on, George. It's a glorious morning. Let's go for an early swim before the pool gets busy. Oh, Georgina. Five days sailing and then - Australia. You'll love it Georgina. Sydney is *fabulous*. It's so alive. So - vibrant. I wouldn't mind living in Australia. Well - in Sydney."

Georgina closed her eyes. Adam was in Sydney. What if she were to see him? He was sure to be on the quayside to meet his sister.

"Thanks Jenny." She sipped the tea thankfully. "It's the best drink of the day, isn't it?"

"Oh, I wouldn't say that,' laughed Jenny. 'I can think of drinks that are much more exciting."

The swimming pool was deserted and the two girls plunged into the cool, exhilarating water. They swam backwards and forwards, revelling in the absence of passengers.

"Hey, Jenny, it's worth getting up early for. We should do this every morning."

"Hm. It depends on what kind of a night I've had. Here's Pete."

"Georgina, Boardroom please. Chop chop."

He turned and walked away without further comment. The two girls left the pool silently, Georgina staring at Jenny questioningly.

"Search me." Jenny shrugged her shoulders, "What have you done now?"

"I - don't know,' Georgina replied, despondently. 'But whatever it is, I'd better go and get it over with. Jenny, why do I seem to spend more time in the Boardroom than anyone else?'

She walked slowly back to her cabin to change into her uniform.

Robert Barnes was waiting for her. "Sit down, Miss Murphy. It seems that you have caused some trouble. Miss Reynolds tells me that because of you, her brother had to leave this ship at Honolulu."

"He - didn't *have* to leave, sir. I would have left."

"Oh, so you admit that you have been bothering Mr Reynolds?"

Georgina remained silent, her eyes lowered.

"You knew the rules. No involvement with passengers. And - I am informed - you threw a drink at him. In full view of everyone. *Answer* me, girl. Did you?"

"I sort of - poured it - sir."

"And is that all you have to say? Miss Murphy, you also told me that you had no encumbrances. You have a child.'

"She isn't an encumbrance. It makes no difference to my work," Georgina replied hotly.

"And what if she had been ill? It happens. Young children do fall ill. You would've wanted to go home. I would've had to send out a replacement. That's why it makes a difference, Miss Murphy. It inconveniences *me*. And - what is more important - it costs the company *money*. I'm disappointed in you. I'm not saying that we wouldn't have employed you, just because you have a child, but you may have been offered a shorter trip. You should have told me. I was going to offer you continuing employment. I shall have to reconsider your position. You may go."

Pete was hovering outside the door. "I'm afraid that Miss Reynolds is taking her revenge for Adam leaving the ship. Sorry, Georgina. I did what I could."

"I know, Pete. Thanks."

Georgina walked away swiftly. A smouldering rage was festering inside her. Not against the company. Not against Robert Barnes. She was sensible enough to know that he had a job to do. And, with hindsight, she realised that he was right. If Rosie *had* been ill, she would have wanted to go home and see her. No, her anger was directed at Eve Reynolds. An overwhelming desire to hurt the woman filled her. And the unfamiliar emotion frightened Georgina. She was aware of her shortcomings. Her passions. Her sometimes uncontrollable temper. But a desire to inflict pain was not one of her failings.

Dave and Jenny were having breakfast on the deck, and they looked up anxiously as Georgina approached them.

"Well," demanded Jenny.

Georgina sat down heavily. "I'll *kill* her. The *bitch.* Why? *Why* has she got it in for me? She didn't have to tell him, did she?"

"What's *happened,* Georgina?"

"Eve Reynolds. She's lost me my job. Barnes won't have me again. He as good as said so. I'm going to see her *now.*" Georgina half stood up.

Both Dave and Jenny reached out and pushed her back down.

"Cool it, idiot. You're playing right into her hands, you little fool."

Jenny called a waiter over. "Full breakfast, please. Now, you're going to sit down and *eat.*"

"I'm going to tell her a few home truths."

"You're doing nothing, Georgina, until you've calmed down." Dave put her cutlery in place. "Your breakfast's on its way. You'll feel better after that."

"Don't bloody patronise me, Dave. I *won't* feel better. Those Reynolds have ruined my life," she cried, dramatically.

"Don't be so stupid,' responded Jenny, calmly. "You shacked up with Reynolds voluntarily. And he obviously hadn't done anything that you disapproved of cos when I saw you, you were like a cat who'd licked the cream."

"Shut up, Jenny.' interjected Dave, uncomfortably. "You're embarrassing the girl."

Jenny, ignoring him, continued. "I warned you about his sort, didn't I? And, after all, Eve Reynolds is a company director. Her two main concerns will be her brother and the company. Why don't you lie low. Keep out of everyone's way for a while. You've a few days yet before we reach Sydney. Perhaps Barnes will change his mind."

Georgina, toying with her food, appeared to have calmed down.

"Perhaps you're right," she said slowly.

"Course we are." Jenny patted her on her shoulder as if pacifying a fretting child. "Now, finish your breakfast then we'll take a quick walk around the deck. You coming, Dave?"

"Sure."

Georgina pushed her plate away. "You two go. I'll have a cup of coffee."

They hesitated, and Georgina grew impatient. "Go *on*. I'm OK."

Dave and Jenny began their walk, blissfully unaware that Georgina's anger had not subsided. That it was her intention to seek out Eve Reynolds as soon as they were out of sight.

Georgina made her way to Eve Reynold's stateroom, and without any hesitation, knocked on the door.

"Come."

The familiar, drawling tone further increased Georgina's wrath. But for once, Georgina's passion was controlled and she entered the cabin, closing the door quietly behind her.

Eve Reynolds, dressed in a pale blue silk dressing gown was sitting at her dressing table, filing her nails. She didn't look up when Georgina entered, as if she had been expecting her.

"Well."

Although the single word was delivered with all the superiority that comes with years of authority of having ones orders obeyed immediately, Georgina was not deterred.

"Thanks to you, Miss Reynolds, my contract will not be renewed. I probably won't be allowed to complete my existing one." Georgina's voice was deceptively soft, belying the turmoil that raged within her.

"I want you to know that, contrary to your belief, I did not 'set my cap' at your brother. I fell in love with him. As you once fell in love with an engineer on a ship."

Eve Reynolds momentarily stopped her filing action, but didn't shift her eyes.

"I didn't want to fall in love. Not with Adam. Not with anyone. You see, Miss Reynolds, as you know, and as you were so eager to tell Adam and Robert Barnes, I have a child. A responsibility. A young life, relying on me for love and support." Georgina's voice became accusing and harsh. Her desire to hurt the woman became overwhelming "Do you know what it's like to have that kind of responsibility? No, Miss Reynolds, you don't. Because you killed your child. And you didn't need to. You'd no financial problems. And you have the audacity to criticise me. Adam was happy with me, Miss Reynolds. But you don't want him to be happy, do you? You want to keep him to yourself. Well, one of these days, he won't want you. No-one will want you. In my book you're a selfish bitch. Bitter and twisted. You're - despicable".

Eve Reynolds stood up and moved towards Georgina, raising her hand, as if to strike her, but Georgina didn't flinch and slowly she dropped her arm to her side.

Turning away from her, she walked to the window and stood with her back to her.

"Who told you about my affair Who told you about the abortion?" she whispered.

Georgina hesitated, unwilling to mention Old Mrs Riley's name.

"It's - common knowledge."

"I think you'd better leave." Eve Reynolds voice was thick with emotion. Georgina turned sharply on her heel and left the cabin.

Chapter Ten

"You're late," hissed Jenny. "Christ, George. You're a glutton for punishment. Fart-face has been wandering around."
The two girls were on coffee duty, and most of the passengers had already been served.
"I told him that you'd nipped out to do an errand for a passenger."
'Thanks, Jenny. You're a pal."
"Where did you go? Are you alright?'
Georgina laughed humourlessly, her anger all spent. "I thought I would feel wonderful, but I don't. I've - been to see Eve Reynolds. I've shot my bolt now anyway. I'll tell you about it later. I'll go and talk to the 'Glums'. I've learned to turn off!"
"There's going to be a barbecue on deck tonight." Dave was umpiring a deck tennis game and Georgina, off duty, was keeping him company. "Join me for dinner, madam?"
Georgina laughed. "It seems so incongruous Dave, to have a barbecue on the high seas."
Dave frowned. "Hmm. I suppose it does. See what I mean about becoming blasé. I never thought of it like that. Anyway," he continued, enthusiastically, "it's a lot of fun. And it's casual dress, which is great."
Georgina had to admit that the constant formal dress required did become a little too much sometimes, and the thought of having dinner in jeans and T-shirt was appealing.
"Hope the weather's OK. We're approaching the Australian bight. It can be a swine sometimes."
"Why's that?' asked Georgina, curiously.
"The ship not only pitches, it rolls from side to side. Most peculiar, I can tell you. It looks pretty settled at the moment. Excuse me, Georgina. That's the game finished I think. See you this evening. We'll make a night of it. Splash out on a bottle of wine."
"Might as well," replied Georgina sadly. "I'll probably be leaving you at Sydney."
"Has Barnes said any more?"
"No, but I had a go at Eve Reynolds.'
Dave sighed. "Why did you *do* it? Was it worth it?"
"No. No, it wasn't. I thought it would have given me a lift, but it

didn't. I feel - pathetic. See you, Dave."

Georgina opened her cabin door and gasped. "What are you doing here? Who let you in? You've no right... "

"Your steward let me in."

Eve Reynolds was standing by the dressing table with Rosie's photograph in her hand. "Is this your little girl?"

Georgina nodded.

"How old is she?"

"Three, nearly four. Listen, it's got nothing to do with you. I'll take that if you don't mind."

Georgina held her hand out for the picture.

Eve Reynolds handed it to her. "Do you miss her?"

"That's a stupid question. Of *course* I do. But no doubt I shall see her shortly. Now, I think you'd better leave." Georgina's tone was sarcastic as she parroted Eve's words.

"Yes. Yes, of course." The woman appeared vague and she sat down on a chair, closing her eyes.

Georgina stared at her. "I say, are you alright?"

"I did kill it, didn't I? I - didn't think of it like that at the time. But you see, my father wouldn't have let me... he said I must..."

Georgina watched in disbelief as the svelte Eve's face crumpled and her body seemed to shrink, like the wicked witch in Wizard of Oz! Georgina, ever fanciful, half expected her to dissolve into a pool of water before her eyes.

"I never forgave myself, you know. Not when I thought about it. But it was too late. And he - the father - had found someone else. So I threw myself into the business. Then when they, our parents, had gone, I looked after Adam. He was going to be married once. He was very young. Only nineteen. The day before the wedding, he found out that she had another lover. A man twice her age. In fact, he had a daughter the same age as her. Adam was devastated. I - suppose I've tried to protect him."

Georgina's thoughts flew back to the first time she had met Adam. The day in the garage when he had as good as accused her of having an affair with the garage proprietor. And she recalled his scathing words. "You're a bit young for him."

Eve picked up the picture again. "She's a beautiful child. A credit to you, Miss Murphy."

Georgina remained silent, and the woman stood up.

"I - should go."

"Yes," said Georgina, firmly.

"Do you mean to say she went into your cabin? That's an intrusion of your privacy. That's not on. You should complain."

Georgina shook her head, wearily. "I can't be bothered, Dave. And I'm not really in a position to complain. It doesn't matter any more. Come on, let's join the queue. The food looks delicious."

The young chefs stood proudly behind the barbeques, handing out succulent, tender steaks, plump sausages, spicy chops, and firm fleshed fish and the waiters filled the plates with salads and fruit. There was an air of festivity on deck, and normally, Georgina would have found the event thrilling.

Dave poured two glasses of wine. "What will you do, Georgina? After this trip, I mean."

Georgina shrugged her shoulders. "Only one thing I can do. Dance. I think I'll get back into a West End show alright. I left without any animosity."

"Will you give me your address? Let me keep in touch, I'd like to keep in touch. And to see Rosie."

Georgina placed her hand over his. "I will. I promise."

He looked at her hand on his. "I'll never forget you, Georgina. I would have liked to try to make you happy."

Georgina removed her hand and smiled. "You keep on saving for those cut glass goblets, Dave. Hey, we're too serious." The band had started to play. "Come on. Let's dance."

The day before the Starlight was due to sail into Sydney harbour, Georgina still didn't know if she was to continue her employment or not.

"You'll have to go and see Barnes," insisted Jenny. "You have a right to know where you stand."

The girls were leaning on the rail of the ship, watching the graceful, acrobatic antics of a school of dolphins when there was a shout from behind them.

"Hey, look. A shark." All that was visible as the beast glided through the water was a triangular shaped, menacing fin."It's after the dolphins."

Georgina shuddered, feeling an affinity with the dolphins as she watched their arctic struggle. Ducking and diving, whilst the shark maintained a steady and seemingly effortless pace behind them. Was this an omen of her battle ahead with Robert Barnes?

She sighed. "You're right, Jenny. I suppose I've been afraid to ask. But yes, I must. I'll do that later on today."

"Do it now," urged Jenny. "See, there's Pete. Go and see him."
Georgina approached Pete gingerly, not sure of her reception.

"Hi, Georgina. Looking forward to Sydney?"

"Pete, how *can* I be? I don't know if I'm in work or not. Can I see Mr Barnes?"

"I'm on my way to meet him now for breakfast. Come and join us."

Pete strode out towards the buffet bar. It was common practise in the glorious weather they were now enjoying to dine on deck whenever possible and even the Captain took advantage of the brilliant sunshine, taking his place in the queue for the self-service breakfast.

"There's Robert. Go and speak to him now."
Georgina walked slowly towards the Entertainment Director and tried a timid smile. His dour face remained expressionless. Georgina's heart sank. He wasn't going to make things easy for her. For a second, she was tempted to turn and walk away.

"Miss Murphy. Come here."

"Yes sir." Georgina was determined to remain polite.

"You may stay on the Starlight to complete your contract - if you wish to do so. After that.. well... we'll have to wait and see. That will be all."

There was an air of expectancy on the ship. They were due to dock early the following morning. The two days stay in Sydney was always the highlight of the cruise. The thrilling sight of the harbour and the first glimpse of Sydney Opera House, was awaited by everyone on the ship with excited anticipation.

"Do you think we shall be able to buy tickets for the opera, Jenny?"

"Doubtful, George, unless you want to pay a hundred pounds. The cheaper tickets are usually sold out weeks in advance. What's on?"

"It's La Boheme. I must try and see it. This will probably be the only chance I have of seeing the Opera House."

"If you feel like standing, you will probably get a ticket."

"Oh, I don't mind that. Will you come with me, Jenny?"

Jenny hesitated. "No. If you don't mind, George. I've already been. Twice. I'll be spending my time in Sydney with Vince."

Georgina was momentarily disappointed. "Ah, well, I'll ask Anna if she will come with me."

"Yes. Yes - you do that."

Georgina sensed some awkwardness in her friends attitude. "Jenny, you are glad I'm staying on, aren't you?"

"Course I am, silly. It's just that... well... I shall be a bit tied up in Sydney. Actually, I wouldn't bother asking Anna either. She has relatives here. On Bondi Beach. She always stays with them. See you."

Georgina was up at six, determined to watch the vessel sail into the harbour. She moved around the cabin quietly, trying not to disturb Jenny. Slipping a jacket around her shoulders, having been warned that it may be cool so early in the morning, Georgina, excitement mounting within her, walked quickly along the gangway and out on to the deck.

There she was met with a sight that made her gasp with sheer delight. Ahead of the ship was the Harbour Bridge, nicknamed the Coathanger by the Australians, and the sheer beauty of it all brought tears to her eyes. In spite of the early hour, the sun was glinting on what has been described as an indisputable wonder of the modern world. Sydney Opera House. The majestic building was everything she had expected and more. Backed by a forest of tall buildings, it stood proud, dwarfing the people milling around the cafes and restaurants fronting it, the epitome of leisure and pleasure. Famous names flooded her mind, falling over themselves to be remembered. Manly Beach, Bondi beach, The Botanical Gardens, Darling Harbour, so many places to see. If only she had someone to share this moment with. Someone like Adam.

Giving herself a mental slap, Georgina told herself that she should be grateful to have this opportunity to be here and not to yearn for something dead and buried.

"What do you think to it?" Georgina turned to see Dave standing behind her

"Dave, it's - indescribable. It's - fantastic, magical and - and wonderful."

"Dave laughed. "You like it, then?"

Georgina remained silent for a few minutes.

"You OK, Georgina?" Dave peered down at her, anxiously.

"Dave, is it my imagination or are people avoiding me?"

Dave looked uncomfortable. "Don't know what you mean," he mumbled.

"In that case, what are *you* doing for the next two days. No-one seems to want to include me in their plans. I'm going to try and get tickets for La Boheme. Will *you* come with me?"

"I'm - not sure yet. I've been to the Opera House once. Let's leave it till we dock and then decide."

Georgina turned away, a little of her pleasure dimmed. There *was* something wrong.

The Starlight sailed gracefully into the natural harbour, the seas and vessel now at one with all the battles over for the time being. She was able to sail in under her own steam, without the aid of tugs, which is one of the features that makes Sydney quite unique. It was at this point, Georgina decided that she would stay away from the side of the ship. She was sure that Adam would be here to meet his sister. If she waited till all the passengers - and Eve - had disembarked, there would be no chance of her seeing him.

She made her way to her cabin. It would take at least an hour before she would be allowed off and in the meantime, she would read about Sydney. Decide where she wanted to go. Convinced now that everyone had made arrangements that didn't include her, she would make the best of it and do her own thing.

"What are you doing in here?" Jenny burst through the door. "We've already docked."

"Jenny, If you don't mind, I'll wait here for a little while."

Jenny stared at her. "What on earth for?"

"I - might see Adam."

"You *won't*. Eve Reynolds is already off the ship. She's a VIP. I saw her. First off, in fact. Anyway, what if you *do* see him? That's all finished isn't it? Bring your things. And by the way, make sure you don't have any food on you. The Australians don't allow anything edible to be taken ashore."

Reluctantly, Georgina gathered together what she thought she would need for the day, and together, the two girls went on deck to watch the activities that were taking place.

There was the disposal of tons of rubbish, fresh water to be taken on, and the restocking of the ship's larders, with all the variety of fresh fruit, fish and meat that Australia has to offer, in addition to hundreds of cases of Australian wine.

"There's Dave and Anna. Let's join them, Georgina."

The two turned and smiled, moving apart to make room for the newcomers.

"What do you think to it all?' Anna was in a conciliatory mood.

"Love it," nodded Georgina.

The quayside was crowded. Young couples with children eagerly waiting to welcome their tearful, but joyful parents who had combined a cruise with a chance to see grandchildren, often for the first time. Old friends meeting after years of separation. Casual spectators whiling away the time, the Australian sunshine being conducive to this pleasurable pastime.

"There's a crowd of Aborigines, Georgina"

Dave pointed to a group of men and women sitting on the floor, one of whom was playing a didgeridoo.

"Look at that child watching them. Look at that gorgeous red hair."

Georgina's gaze followed the direction of Anna's pointing finger and her heart skipped a beat. The little girl, standing with her back to the ship had hair the same colour as Rosie's. And then the child turned around to speak to the woman standing beside her. Georgina began to shake. The blood pounded in her head and her legs turned to jelly. It *was* Rosie. It was Rosie and her mother. She turned to her smiling friends.

"I don't believe it. How... when... that's my little girl."

Jenny held out the bag, containing the Hawaiian outfit she and Anna had bought for Rosie.

"Took this out of your drawer. Off you go, Georgina. Give her it with all our love."

Georgina gasped. "You *knew.* You *all* knew. That's why you wouldn't make arrangements to go out with me. Oh, you're all *wonderful.*" She flung her arms around them, gathering them all together closely.

"They've seen you. See, she's waving."

Georgina took the bag from Jenny and, ignoring the shouts of the officers who were dispatching the passengers in an orderly manner, sped along the deck and down the gangway to her waiting family.

Her three friends watched her, and Anna surreptitiously dabbed her eyes.

"Is that a tear I see?" asked Jenny, waspishly.

"Don't be bloody stupid. I've got a piece of grit in my eye!"

"Oh Lord." Dave groaned. "Jenny, do you see who I see?"

"Oh Christ. Not Reynolds."

"Look. Over there." Jenny followed Dave's pointing finger.

Jenny gasped. "I don't believe it. That rat-bag Jock Campbell."

Chapter Eleven

After an emotional reunion, the excited conversion between Georgina, her mother and Rosie caused bystanders to turn and smile sympathetically. The child hopped from one foot to the other, pulling at Georgina's skirt. Georgina lifted her high into the air, showing herto her three friends who were still waiting to disembark.

"Miss Murphy, may I have a word with you?"

Georgina turned sharply. Eve Reynolds, her elegance restored, stood beside her.

She spoke to Georgina's mother. "Kathleen, would you give us a few minutes?"

"Come on, Rosie," said Kathleen, cheerfully. "Lets go and watch the ferry boats."

Georgina stared at Eve Reynolds, bemused. "How do you know my mother's name?"

"I arranged for them to be here, Georgina. I'm trying to make amends."

"How did you get them here so quickly?" demanded Georgina.

Eve laughed dryly "A company director of a shipping line can arrange almost anything."

"Why are you doing this for me? Please, don't pretend now that you *like* me."

The woman ignored Georgina's sarcastic tone. "I've arranged for your mother and Rosie to stay in my flat."

"I... we don't need any favours."

"Don't be stupid, Georgina." Eve Reynolds spoke sharply. "Can you afford for them to stay in a hotel?"

"We'll manage," replied Georgina, stiffly.

The two women stared at one another defiantly, then Eve sighed.

"Please, Georgina," she said softly. "Let me do this. It's for my benefit too." She laughed nervously. "Ease my conscience a bit, perhaps. Listen, spend the day with them. And tonight, I have tickets for you and Kathleen for the opera. It's La Boheme. I'm sure you'd want to see it. I'll take care of Rosie. That is - if you can trust me with her."

Georgina looked deep into the woman's eyes, that were suddenly filled with anxiety, as Adams had been when he'd had asked her if she wanted him to love her.

She hesitated for a second. “Yes,” she whispered. “Of course I can trust you.”

Eve breathed deeply. “Right.” She was her brisk, confident self again. “Off you go. And, Georgina, I’ve asked Captain to let you take Kathleen and Rosie on board. You can give them a guided tour.”

Eve Reynolds turned to leave.

“Miss Reynolds“

“Yes?”

Georgina had been going to inquire if she had seen her brother yet, but decided that it was a pointless question. Adam wouldn’t want to see her ever again.

“Nothing. I mean... what - should I wear at the opera?” she finished, lamely.

“Is this where you sleep, mummy? Can I climb on your bed? Will you show me where you dance, mummy? Can I go on a ship when I’m a big girl?”

Georgina and Kathleen laughed at the torrent of questions pouring from Rosie’s lips.

“It’s time you and granny went. I’m on duty for a couple of hours. Not everyone leaves the ship, you know, so there are passengers that we have to take care of. Mum, I’ll see you at the Opera House. Rosie, you’ll be a good girl for Miss Reynolds, won’t you?”

“Of *course* I will,” Rosie replied, indignantly. “And it’s not Miss Reynolds. It’s Aunty Eve.”

Georgina looked at her mother, questioningly, and Kathleen nodded, shrugging her shoulders.

“Georgina, you’d better take your ticket for the opera. If there’s a crowd waiting to go in I may not see you. Come along Rosie, let mummy go to work.”

Georgina hummed to herself as she poured out tea and passed around scones and cream cakes.

“Are you not going ashore, Mrs Moody?”

The Glums were sitting looking out of the window. “It’s too busy.”

“Yes, it’s too busy.”

Georgina sat down beside them. “Why don’t you give it a try?” she asked gently. “Why don’t you take the ferry to Manly Beach? Have you ever been there?”

The pair shook their heads.

"They say it's lovely. If you like, I'll come to the ferry boat with you." She could see them weakening, "I'll get your tickets for you," she urged.

"Alright." They stood up simultaneously.

Georgina couldn't believe it. She motioned Pete to come over to her.

"Pete, may I slip out for a few minutes? Mr and Mrs Moody are going to Manly Beach."

Pete tried not to look surprised. "Certainly you can, Miss Murphy. You're a bloody genius, Georgina," he said under his breath as he walked away.

Georgina took her cream silk suit out of the wardrobe. She hadn't worn it since the night she and Adam had had dinner in his cabin. She held it to her face, remembering how Adam had unfastened the tiny pearl buttons with fingers so sensitive, she'd hardly felt them. But she'd felt them when she had stood naked in front of him. Gentle, searching, over her body, her face, through her hair and touching her lips. She was convinced that she could still smell the masculine scent of him, lingering on the dress.

"Don't be stupid, Georgina," she told herself, firmly.

She dressed quickly and released her hair from its clips that held it back. It fell softly on to her shoulders. Her skin had tanned beautifully and she knew she had never looked better than she did this evening.

As she stepped out towards the Opera House, the warmth of the evening sun on her face, Georgina couldn't believe that she was in Australia, walking along Circular Quay, on her way to Sydney Opera House. And the icing on the cake was to have Rosie and her mother here, albeit just for a couple of days. She didn't dare hazard a guess how much Eve Reynolds had paid for them to travel here.

Looking at her watch, she anxiously increased her pace. Sorting out the Glums' tickets for the ferry had taken longer than she'd expected. She smiled as she thought of them. She was sure they'd been quite excited.

The opera started at seven. She put on an extra spurt. Her mother, ever punctual, and whom she knew would already be in her seat, would be starting to worry. Running up the stairs, Georgina found her door and took the ticket out of her pocket. She glanced at it, then gasped as she realised that they were to sit in the hundred pound seats.

Her frugal nature came to the surface and, horrified, she thought "What a terrible waste of money. We could have stood for ten pounds."

And she laughed as she tried to imagine the Miss Reynolds standing at the back of the auditorium in those incredibly high heels of hers.

"This way, madam."
Dismayed, Georgina realised that her mother hadn't arrived. Perhaps Rosie had been playing up. She was well aware that she could be quite a little madam when she wanted.

The Opera was due to start in five minutes time and Georgina continued to glance around her anxiously. The warning bell rang and still there was no sign of Kathleen. If she didn't arrive within the next few seconds, she wouldn't be allowed in until after the first interval.
The lights lowered. Georgina had to content herself and stop looking around. The music started and it was with relief that Georgina sensed a movement beside her.

"You're late," she whispered, watching the curtain rise.

"Sorry, Irish."
Georgina caught her breath and then, with a deep, quivering sigh, tentative placed her hand on his knee, smiling as he gently covered it with his own.
For the next half hour, they both sat in deep contentment, holding hands, sharing a common love of music, secure in the knowledge that they were going to spend the rest of their lives together.

When the lights went up for the first interval, they turned to one another and smiled.

"Forgiven?" Adam enquired, pleadingly.
Georgina lilted her face and kissed him lightly on his lips. "Forgiven."

"Georgina, could you bear to miss the rest of the opera?"
Georgina smiled at him, mischievously. "Did you have something else in mind, Adam?"

"Come on, minx. Let's get out of here."

As they walked to the exit, Georgina hesitated. "Adam, there's a couple standing at the back. Do you mind if I ask them if they want our seats?'
Adam laughed. "If you want to."

"It's just that I can't bear to think of all that money going to waste."

"Oh, my darling girl. I'm going to have a wonderful time teaching you how to spend money without feeling guilty. Go on. Tell them to take the seats."
She returned, satisfied, and they left the building, running down the stairs like children let out of school at the end of term.

Adam poured two glasses of wine and handed one to her. She sipped it, gratefully. "Thanks, Adam. This is a lovely apartment. How often do you

use it?"
"Probably three, four times a year. Never mind that now. Come here, Georgina. Put that glass down."
Georgina felt the blood rushing to her head as he looked at her, desire burning in his eyes. And she responded willingly, eagerly, to his need. Slowly, unselfconsciously she began to unfasten the tiny pearl buttons on her suit. He touched her lips with his fingers.
"You do the rest, Adam."
Their eyes locked, hypnotised, as his fingers carefully unfastened the buttons and he slowly removed the top of her suit. She unzipped her skirt, stepping out of it gracefully and turned around for him to release her bra.
"I'd almost forgotten how lovely you are, Georgina."
He undressed and, sweeping her into his arms, carried her to the bedroom. "No." He shook his head. "That's not true. I couldn't forget. Georgina, I've thought of nothing else but you. Darling, I love you so much." He lowered her gently on his bed and looked down on her.
"I'm so sorry, Georgina. That night on the ship. Forgive me. It was a terrible thing to say to you."
"It's alright, Adam."
She smiled and held her arms out to him, and with a hoarse cry, he took her in his arms. Their bodies moved in intense loving and pleasurable unison and she ran her fingers through his hair as he kissed her breasts.
"Darling Adam, let this moment last for ever."
As they lay with limbs entwined, passion spent, and in mutual satisfaction, Georgina knew that she had to know how he felt about Rosie. Loosening herself from his embracing arms, she asked hesitantly.
"Adam, how do you feel about my little girl? You know I could never give her up."
"What on earth are you talking about, Georgina? Do you think I would ask you to do that? I've had time to think whilst I've been here on my own. I was wrong, Georgina. I realise with hindsight that you must have started to tell me about Rosie so many times. I'm asking you again to marry me. And I want to adopt Rosie. She'll be our child and I'll love her as if she were my own flesh and blood."
"You don't know her, Adam. You've never even seen her."
He smiled at her. "I know her mother. That's good enough for me."
Laughing, he said, "Anyway, Georgina, I've been given the go ahead from

sister Eve. And that's praise indeed for you."

"And what if she'd not approved Adam?' asked Georgina, seriously. "What then?"

"It wouldn't have made any difference. Eve thinks that she controls me. It's suited me to let her think that. But nothing now would keep me from you, my darling. Without you, my life has no meaning."

"Adam, do you know what I want at this moment, more than anything else in the whole world?"

He rolled over on top of her. "You're a wicked, insatiable harlot."

She pushed him away and sat up. "I'm not. I'm starving. Adam, after all the rich food I've had on the Starlight, I want some fish and chips. Please let's go out and find some."

"Would you like to go on a boat today, Rosie?"

Georgina and Adam had returned to Eve's flat for breakfast. Rosie stared at Adam with innocent unblinking eyes.

"I can't go anywhere with strangers, thank you very much."

"Your mummy will be with you too."

"Can Aunty Eve come too? And Granny?"

Adam laughed. "That sounds fine to me. Eve?"

"Look, how about letting me look after Rosie for a few hours. We'll go to Manly Beach. Give us a chance to get to know one another. You three can stay here and have a chat and then lunch. There's plenty of food and drink in the fridge. Your mum can give my brother the once over. I'm sure she will be wondering what you're letting yourself in for, Georgina."

"Georgina?"

Georgina hesitated. After such a long time away from her child, she wanted to spend as much time as possible with her.

"*Please.*"

"She will look after her, you know." Adam spoke quietly.

"You promise to behave, Rosie?" Georgina smiled at the little girl, now hopping impatiently from one foot to the other.

"I'm always good, aren't I granny? And I'll wear my new hula-hula skirt."

"Oh no you wont," Georgina said firmly.

Rosie sighed deeply and, standing feet apart and hands on hips, defiantly geared herself up for a battle. Adam suppressed a chuckle, as he recognised a stance reminiscent of Georgina.

Rosie, sensing a sympathiser, moved closer to Adam. "Oh yes I..." She stopped suddenly as her mother fixed her with a steely glint in her eye.

Rosie, acquiescing immediately, stretched her hand out to Eve and, mimicking her granny's Irish brogue said, "Come on, me darlin. Let's be goin."

As the pair left the flat, Adam roared with laughter."Oh Lord, Kathleen. I don't know about *you* wondering what Georgina's letting herself in for. I'm beginning to wonder what *I'm* letting myself in for."

Georgina stood looking out of the window of Eve's flat admiring the panoramic view of the Sydney Cove. Dozens of tiny vessels bobbed up and down, surrounding the cruise liner, Starlight, cosily tucked away in her berth looking peaceful and at rest, but Georgina could by now imagine the hive of activity going on inside her. Cabins would be being cleaned out ready for the next intake of passengers, food stores re-stocked, waste disposed of. New entertainers arriving for the next stage of the journey. She thought fleetingly of Hugh Campbell but quickly dismissed him. Hopefully, she would never see him again.

The Opera House was in her view, with hundreds of people milling around and others sitting by the water front. Cafes were busy serving diners and over head an electric railway and an expressway dominated the Quay, from whose jetties the ferryboats plied, taking tourists to various beaches and also ferrying workers to and from their places of work.

She could see a piper, dressed in Scottish ensemble, surrounded by photographers, playing the bagpipes and once again, her thoughts were on Hugh Campbell. Deep down, there was a reluctant admission that now that he was aware of Rosie's existence, he could claim access rights. But again, she quickly dismissed such thoughts. Nothing was going to spoil the happiness she felt today.

"More coffee, Adam?"

Georgina smiled to herself as she heard her mum speak, knowing from the tone of her voice that she thoroughly approved of him. And Adam liked her mum. She could see he was completely at ease with her. And Eve? All that planning with her mum to get her and Adam together at the opera. Kathleen had obviously taken at once to Eve. She usually liked to take her time to get to know new acquaintances, protecting their privacy jealously. But they were behaving as if they were
old friends. She sighed contentedly. All was well with Georgina's world.

"Adam. Telephone."

He was in the kitchen clearing the dishes much to Kathleen's delight. She handed the phone to him."I think it's Eve. She sounds a bit odd."

Georgina was immediately on the alert and walked across to join Adam.

"What is it, Adam?" she whispered.

"Sh," he said. "OK Eve, stay where you are. We'll be right with you."

"What is it. Is something wrong?" Georgina grabbed his arm. "Tell me."

"Kathleen." Adam's voice was grim. "You stay here. Stay by the phone. Georgina, come with me. We're going to Manly."

"Adam, for God's sake. What's happened. Is it Rosie. Is she hurt. Oh I should never have let her go."

"She's gone. Eve can't find her."

Chapter Twelve

By the time Adam and Georgina reached Manly Harbour, Eve had contacted the police, who were starting to question members of the public.

"Do you have any photographs, Sir? Miss Reynolds here has given us a description and has told us what the child is wearing."

Adam looked questioningly at Georgina.

She nodded numbly. "In my bag." Fumbling around desperately, she produced two. "They're recent. Just before I left."

She began to cry, heart rending sobs racking her body. "Oh Adam. I'm so frightened. My poor baby. Where is she?"

"Stop that, Georgina." He shook her by the shoulders. "We'll find her."

Eve put her arms around her. "I'm so sorry, Georgina. I turned away for a second and she was gone."

"Excuse me." A policeman approached them bringing with him a young woman. "This lady here says she saw a child being led away rather quickly by a man. Will you let her see a photo?"

Georgina handed her a picture, anxiously watching her reaction.

"Yes - yes. that's her. That hair. Unmistakable, isn't it?"

Georgina shouted to her angrily. "Why didn't you stop him? Surely..."

"Georgina, stop it, will you?" Adam spoke sharply. "This will get us nowhere."

"Turning to the woman, he spoke softly to her. "What did the man look like? Did he say anything?"

"Actually, I *did* stop him cos it looked a bit odd. And he looked as if he'd been drinking but he said he was her daddy. And... well... she looked a bit like him. You know. The hair. He had red hair." She frowned. "And... ah yes. He spoke with - I think - a Scottish accent".

Georgina's heart began to pound. Her head was spinning so much she had to hold on to Adam to stop herself falling.

"Oh God, Adam. It's Hugh. Hugh Campbell. He must have been following us."

The young woman spoke again "I'm so sorry. I didn't know, did I? The little girl didn't seem to be frightened. She said they were going to see some sharks."

"He's going to kill her," Georgina gasped. "He'll throw her in the sea. He's doing it to punish me."

"Don't be stupid Georgina," snapped Adam.

"You don't know him," said Georgina breathlessly "When he's drunk, he'll do any thing."

"Adam." Eve spoke urgently. "*Sharks.*"

Adam looked askance at her for a few seconds, then they spoke unison.

"Marineland."

"Come on." Adam grabbed Georgina's hand and they ran along the esplanade, followed by Eve and the policeman, trailed by the young woman and another policeman, leaving behind them an excited and bemused crowd of onlookers, amongst whom rumour ran rife that there was a school of sharks lurking in Sydney Cove and that at least one swimmer had been gobbled up.

Marineland was packed with enthusiasts, the most popular attraction being the feeding of the fifteen foot grey nurse shark. Georgina, searching frantically amongst the crowds called out Rosie's name over and over again. Adam, that much taller than most, pushed his way to the front, and, standing there, totally absorbed in the great creature thrashing around was Rosie. Behind her was Hugh Campbell. Adam strode forward and swooped Rosie up into his arms.

"Move, Campbell," he said menacingly. "Over here."

As they reached Georgina, she slowly lifted her hand, clenched her fist and hit him.

He staggered and almost fell.

"Now - leave us alone, Hugh." she said quietly.

Rosie began to cry. "I'm sorry mummy."

Eve bent down and picked her up. "Come with me, sweetheart. Adam, come away. Leave them alone for a while."

"Georgina, I wouldn't have hurt her. I just - wanted to see her."

The policeman walked over to them. "You OK Miss. Do you know this man? Do you want to press any charges?"

Georgina shook her head. "No, it's alright. Thanks. He - is her father."

"And what about you, Sir. That was quite a punch. You OK."

An embarrassed Hugh Campbell rubbed his chin. "No - no, it was nothing. Hardly felt a thing."

"Even so, young lady, you can't go around hitting people, causing a public nuisance."

Georgina opened her mouth to respond angrily but swiftly realised that she was in no position to antagonise the law. "I'm so sorry officer. It wont happen again."

The officer walked away and rejoined his colleague. "Phew," he remarked. "For a little 'un she really does pack a punch."

"Georgina. I promise. I wont ever bother either of you again. It was a stupid thing to do. What about Reynolds? Are you going to marry him?"

"If he still wants me. I've been nothing but trouble to him" Georgina sighed. "I love him, Hugh. I really and truly love him."

"Will you let me know about Rosie from time to time, Georgina. You know. The odd photo perhaps?"

She nodded. "I suppose so. You're her father, Hugh. You're entitled."

"Adam, why don't you three spend the morning on the yacht? I'd really like to take Kathleen shopping. She's seen nothing of Sydney yet." Eve turned to Kathleen. "I must show you The Queen Victoria Building. It's been so beautifully restored and then we'll go to Paddy's Market. There's about a thousand stalls there."

"Yes. I'd like that. I do love a market. So many bargains to be found."
The thought of the elegant Eve wandering around a market looking for a bargain tickled Georgina and she burst out laughing.

"That's better." Adam beamed. "It's good to see you happy again, darling. Now Rosie, would you like to see Aunty Eve's yacht? I think the captain may let you sail her."

"Is it as big as mummy's boat and what colour is it and what's it called?" asked Rosie.

"No, it's not as big as Starlight and it's blue and it's called..." he glanced questioningly at Eve.
She nodded.

"It... *she...* is going to be re-christened - 'The Rosie'. Right. Shall we do that? All agreed?"
Everyone nodded.

"That would be wonderful, Adam. Thank you," smiled Georgina.

It was late afternoon when they all arrived back at the flat. The yachters agreed they'd had a glorious time sailing from Manly Harbour to explore Darling Harbour, finishing with a quick call to Bondi beach. Kathleen said she had never seen such wonderful market and that the Queen Victoria Building had indeed been well restored, even though she`d never seen the original and that Eve would make a great tour guide, a comment which Adam seemed to find highly amusing.

The four adults sat contentedly sipping aperitifs while Rosie sat at Georgina's feet looking at a picture book bought from Paddy's Market.

"Georgina, hadn't you better start thinking about taking your luggage off Starlight. She sails tonight."

There was a long silence. Rosie, ever sensitive to an atmosphere, stared at each adult in turn.

"What do you mean, Adam?"

"Well, as Eve has invited Kathleen and Rosie to stay in Australia for a while, we may as well use the opportunity and get married here. It can be arranged."

"I - can't do that, Adam."

"Why ever not?"

He caught the determined glint in Georgina's eyes and groaned. "Don't tell me."

Georgina nodded, "I'm going back on the ship, Adam. I intend completing my contract."

It was Adam's turn to stare. He looked questioningly at Kathleen, who shrugged her shoulders, helplessly. He turned to Eve.

"Don't look at me, Adam. I've interfered enough in Georgina's working life. It's entirely up to her. Anyway, I can understand her wanting to prove herself in this job, and in fact, I admire her for it."

He turned to Rosie. "Well Rosie, shall we let your mummy go back on the ship?`

"Are you going to be my daddy?"

Adam turned to Georgina for help.

"Rosie," began Georgina, gently, "the man who took you to see the sharks. That was your daddy. But... well - he can't really look after you, so Adam is going to be your - Pop."

She looked questioningly to Adam who nodded his agreement.

"That's alright then. You can stay with me while mummy's working."

"Looks as if I'm outnumbered. Kathleen, can you have a wedding dress made for when the ship docks in Southampton?" He smiled at Rosie. "And a bridesmaid dress? What colour Rosie?"

"Blue please. Like my ship."

"Where are we going tonight, Adam?"

Eve had taken Kathleen for a drive around the area, ostensibly to let her see a bit more of Sydney but Adam and Georgina gratefully acknowledging it was to give them some time to themselves.

Adam, lifting a sleepy Rosie in his arms said, "Shall we get this little one to bed first. You know, Eve's going to spoil her rotten. I hope Kathleen isn't going to mind if she wants to look after her from time to time.

Georgina laughed. "You don't know my mother. As soon as I'm able to look after Rosie myself, she will be up and away and doing her own thing. She says she has a lot of living to do yet."

"Right. As soon as the wanderers return, we'll pick up a blanket from my apartment. I've arranged for the delicatessen to put a picnic together for us."

Although the evening was warm as Georgina and Adam made their way to the Botanical Gardens, Adam had warned her to take a woollen jumper with her.

"How long is it going to take us to eat this picnic?' laughed Georgina.

"This is a special night, Georgina. Wait and see. Here's a spot. Spread out the blanket and I'll see what's in the basket.'

He brought out a selection of mouth watering delicacies. Plover's eggs, vol au vents, two kinds of pate and crisp rolls, a pot of red caviar and - a bottle of champagne.

"First things first. We'll drink this before it gets warm." He opened the bottle and, digging deep into the picnic basket, produced two cut glass goblets.

Georgina smiled a little sadly as she thought of Dave and their picnic on the beach at Waikiki. There would be no plastic beakers for Adam. He poured the sparkling liqueur and handed a glass to her.

"To us, my darling. Together - forever."

Georgina looked around her. The ground was beginning to fill up. Couples, large parties, all with blankets and picnics.

"What is happening, Adam? So many people here, all with blankets." She laughed. "Adam - it's not an *orgy*, is it?"

"Not - quite, my darling, it's, - A MID SUMMER NIGHT'S DREAM."

As he spoke, the Shakespearian company emerged, and there began for Georgina, a night of magic. She sat in a dream, transported to a world of fairies. Oberon and Titania, Pease blossom, Cobweb, Mustard seed and Moth, Bottom, Snug and Snout and all the other characters who help to make the play such sheer delight. As the fairy grotto became ablaze with bright sparkling lights, blue and orange and purple and red and as Puck swung from tree to tree, Georgina looked at her watch.

"Adam, the Starlight sails in two hours. I'll have to go soon."
He whispered in her ear and with a sweet smile Georgina stood up and held out her hand to him. Adam gathered up the blanket and they moved away from the crowds.

They lay together under the starry midnight blue sky, listening to the faint voices of the actors.

"Did you hear what Theseus said, Adam? "She will find him by starlight. Here she comes - and her passion ends the play." Love me before I have to leave, Adam. Let's make this *our* Midsummer Night's Dream."

THE END